# Books by Keely Brooke Keith

## THE UNCHARTED SERIES

*The Land Uncharted*

*Uncharted Redemption*

*Uncharted Inheritance*

*Christmas with the Colburns*

*Uncharted Hope*

*Uncharted Journey*

*Uncharted Destiny*

*Uncharted Promises*

*Uncharted Freedom*

*Uncharted Courage*

## THE UNCHARTED BEGINNINGS SERIES

*Aboard Providence*

*Above Rubies*

*All Things Beautiful*

# Uncharted Inheritance

## Keely Brooke Keith

Edenbrooke
Press

Cover designed by Najla Qamber Designs
Edited by Dena Pruitt
Interior design by Edenbrooke Press
Author photo courtesy of Frank Auer

Printed in the United States of America
ISBN: 9781092502511

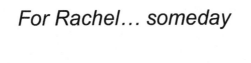

*For Rachel… someday*

# Chapter One

Bethany Colburn panted as she ran down the forest path away from the shore. Her heels sank into the loose sand between the fallen gray leaf twigs, and her legs burned from the weight of her boots. Ahead, a wisp of smoke rose from the chimney of her family's home. She was almost there. The cramp in her side demanded she stop running, but shock compelled her forward.

As she rounded the medical cottage and rushed toward the Colburn house, Connor stepped out the back door. She nearly ran into him and sucked in a breath. "You won't believe what I saw at the shore! Come quickly!"

Connor held up a hand, exuding the calm of a man used to her demonstrative announcements. "Slow down. Take a deep breath. Okay?"

Bethany hummed an exhalation and hoped that proved the composure he requested. "Okay," she replied, using his vernacular.

Connor nodded. "What did you see?"

"Some big metal thing from the outside world. I think it's a machine. It's not like anything we have in the Land."

"A big metal thing? Does it look like the space debris we found last year?"

"No." She caught her breath, but her pulse was still pounding in her ears. "It's old and rusted."

"Out here?" Connor pointed east.

"No. Farther south—below the bluffs."

"On the shore?"

"Yes, well, in the shallow caves below the bluffs. I went down there at low tide because I need potash to make the black glaze for all the orders I have at the pottery yard, and I went farther back into the clefs of the rock than I normally go and that's where I saw it. It's buried in the rock." She bent to rub her aching calf muscle. "It's in the sediment beneath the bluffs."

"An old, rusted machine?"

"Yes, and it has a window and I think I saw bones inside it. Most of it is buried in the rock, but it's huge whatever it is."

"Keep your voice down." Connor patted the air as if that would allay her. "Show me where it is, but be cool about it."

"Cool?"

He nodded then glanced at the road when a wagon passed by. After waving at the driver, Connor put his hand on Bethany's back and shepherded her toward the path to the beach. "Stay calm so you don't raise suspicion. If it's been there awhile, we aren't in any danger. Right?"

"I guess not."

"Right, so be cool." He looked behind them as they stepped onto the path toward the shore. "How far is it?"

"About a mile."

"A mile? What did you say you were doing down there?"

"I went at low tide to the caves where Mrs. Vestal and I get the minerals we use in pottery recipes, but the waves must have eroded more of the bluff since last time I was there. I couldn't find potash in our normal spot, so I went back into the caves a bit and that's when I saw it—"

"The machine with a window and bones inside it?"

"Right." Bethany stayed on the hard packed sand as she and Connor walked along the shore below the bluffs. The roar of the waves echoed off the rock, making it sound as though the ocean were on both sides of her. With the tide still out, the shallow caves and murky pools below the rocky cliff face made her feel small. If they were trapped there when the tide came back in, they would be caught in the current and swept out to sea—just like Luke and Walter had been. The three-year-old memory made the skin along her spine crawl as she looked out at the waves. "It won't be long until the tide turns."

Connor glanced at her. "We'll be fine. I won't let anything happen to you."

Bethany mustered a grin, grateful for his reassurance. As she walked close to the rocks, an eerie feeling made her belly sink. She wanted to turn back and run home. Instead, she folded her arms over her chest and kept walking.

Connor's brow furrowed. "Are you all right?"

Bethany couldn't answer. She bent to pick up the pail and trowel she had dropped in her panicked flight when she first saw the machine. Then she pointed at the dark clef behind a section of coppery brown rock. "It's in there."

She stayed back while Connor walked between the walls of jagged rock. He wiped away sand, exposing more of the window and rusted metal. "Whoa!" He smiled as he glanced back at her. "Yep, you found a skeleton." He reached out for her trowel. Gripping the tool with both hands, he scraped along the metal of the machine. "This plane is called a Hellcat—"

"A what?"

"No, wait," he retracted his assessment as he chipped away more flaky sediment. "It's a Wildcat. See the wing would have been up here—higher than the Hellcat—but the wing is missing."

"The wing?" Bethany stepped closer. "That machine is an airplane?"

"Yeah, it's an old fighter plane from the Second World War."

"How many have there been?"

"World Wars?"

"Yes."

"Including the current war—three. I taught about that in history last year, remember?" He kicked sand away from the bottom of the airplane and pointed to a faded insignia on the metal. "Looks like it was Royal Navy. What was a Martlet doing way out here?" He curved his hand and peered through the window. "The pilot is still wearing his helmet. Wow, look at those old gauges and the radio. He's got a portable transmitter in there. Man, I would love to know his story. What a relic!" Connor's voice was muffled against the glass. He pulled away. "Do you want to take a look?"

"You are enjoying this, aren't you?"

When he only wiggled his eyebrows, Bethany touched the window and looked inside the darkened capsule. In front of the skeletal remains of the pilot was a panel indented with several circular instruments. A black rod protruded between the pilot's knees. Crusted straps covered his decayed clothing remnants. Her stomach lurched when she saw the curve of his neck bones. She backed away. "How long do you think he's been here?"

Connor put his hands on his hips and glanced around the rock. "These airplanes were retired in nineteen forty-five, so at least eighty years. He must have crashed into the ocean and floated here. The wings are gone, at least the one on this side. Somehow, the fuselage remained intact and was washed into the cave. The sediment helped seal him in." Connor looked back at the sea then motioned to her pail. "Did you get your soil?"

"Hm?"

"The minerals you needed for the pottery?"

"No."

He handed her back the trowel. "Go dig some up before the tide comes back. We'll have to get out of here soon."

Bethany stepped around the shallow pools of water that were fed by the runoff from the bluffs above. The minerals from the decayed vegetation would provide the potash she needed. Connor stayed by the old airplane and looked in its window while she stepped into an open cave and bent to the ground. She glanced over her shoulder continually, unable to focus on the soil. After only gathering one scoop, she picked up her pail and hurried back. "What are you going to do with the airplane… and with the pilot?"

Connor was still staring in the airplane's window. "I would like to remove the window and get inside the cockpit, but the tide will come in soon. He is sealed in there really well, so I don't want to open it until I'm prepared to get everything out and take it to higher ground. I'll have to come back with Levi—maybe tomorrow. We'll bury the pilot's remains, of course, but we may leave the aircraft here. It hasn't hurt anything by being here all these years, but I don't want people down here." Connor brushed the dirt off his hands and ushered her away from the rocks. "Listen, Beth, you have to keep this to yourself."

The find was unsettling, but it didn't seem like something to keep secret like a hurtful indiscretion or a sinful longing. She glanced back at the yellowed glass of the window and shuddered, knowing a dead man was inside. "Why can't I tell anyone?"

Connor took the pail and carried it for her. "We don't want kids playing on it and getting hurt or curious villagers getting trapped here when the tide comes in. Plus, there may be weapons onboard or equipment that could put the Land at risk."

"Can I tell Father?"

"I'll tell him."

"What about Lydia?"

"Let me decide who to tell. Okay?"

As they reached the grass that mingled in the loose white sand, Bethany looked back at the bluffs and the wreckage, which was now obscured by the crenulated rocks. No one ever went there but her. No one would know about the old airplane, except whomever Connor chose to tell. She could trust him. "Okay," she whispered as she turned her face toward home.

* * *

Bethany flinched when sparks popped out of the settling bonfire. She chuckled at herself, then she moved her legs away from the log she was sitting on and buried her feet in the powdery sand. The breaking waves hummed on the shore behind her, lulling her back into her reverie. She reached down and traced the outline of her feet in the sand.

Everett Foster was whistling a melody Bethany did not recognize as he came out of the forest near the historic cairn. He carried an armload of broken branches to their dwindling fire. His dark hair swooped across his forehead. He immediately flipped it out of his eyes and smiled at her. "We can't let the fire die this early on our last night of summer."

Connor skipped a clamshell across the shallows as he walked toward the bonfire and sat beside Lydia on the far end of the group's log bench. The makeshift seat moved beneath Bethany. Connor leaned his elbows onto his knees and grinned. "How come I'm the only one who has school tomorrow?"

"Because you are the teacher," Lydia answered as she rested her head on Connor's shoulder. She yawned. "I should go home and check on the baby."

"You just want to go to bed." Connor rubbed Lydia's back. "Don't worry about the baby; Andrew is fine with his grandpa."

A quiet but ever-present yearning kept Bethany staring at her sister and brother-in-law. Firelight warmed their contours as Lydia twined her finger in the edge of Connor's shirt and he kissed the top of her head. And in one heartbeat, beneath the stars and the oval moon, Bethany decided all of life's happiness hinged on being loved by a man like Connor.

While Everett fed the fire, Levi and Mandy sat on the other end of the log. They nestled close to one another. Levi sighed with contentment as Mandy tucked herself against his chest. Then he looked past Bethany and said to Connor, "Tell us one of your stories."

"You just want him to frighten me," Mandy protested weakly. She twirled a strand of auburn hair and winked at Bethany.

"Maybe I do." Levi smiled down at Mandy. As they started to kiss, Bethany forced herself to politely look away from her brother and his wife.

Everett prodded the fire with the last stick from his bundle. The flames licked at the fresh kindling and danced into crisp peaks of orange light. He held onto his poker stick as he backed away from the crackling fire. Then he motioned to the slice of empty space on the log beside Bethany. "Scoot down a bit, Beth."

She moved closer to Lydia to make room for Everett. The log bench dropped a degree as he sat beside her. She liked being close to him. She felt safe and loved beside him, but not in the way Connor loved Lydia or the way Levi loved Mandy. She glanced at Everett. "What was that tune you were whistling?"

"Just a new song I've been working on." He put his arm behind her. While they waited for

Connor to tell one of his scary stories from the outside world, Bethany leaned into Everett's side and wondered if Connor had told Lydia or Levi about the old airplane yet.

"Have you heard the one about the couple who went out on a date one night?" Connor shifted toward the group. No one replied. Of course they hadn't. "While the guy was driving his date around town in his car, they were listening to music on the car radio. Between songs, a news bulletin came on the radio about a vicious murderer who had escaped from prison. The reporter said the murderer was a psychopath that slashed his victims to pieces and he could be easily identified because instead of a right hand he had a rusty hook—the very hook he used to kill his victims." Connor held up his forearm and curled his fingers for effect. "When the girl heard the report, she scooted close to the guy because she was scared, but he got the wrong idea and decided to drive out to the country. As soon as they got out of town, he pulled the car over in the woods. He turned off the car engine and moved close to her when suddenly there was a loud scratching sound on the back of the car. Screech! Then again—screech! Over and over." Connor gestured a hook-hand scratching at the air while he spoke. Bethany's mouth dropped open as she listened. She promptly closed it and looked at the fire, trying to think of something else. She imagined a carriage without horses and music coming from something called a radio. As she began to ponder an unmarried man and woman alone at night in the woods, the fright of the possible murder dissipated. She wondered what it would be like to be alone with a man, what it was like to ride in a car, and what happened to the murderer's hand that made him need a hook.

Connor continued, "So the guy tried to start the car's engine to leave, but it wouldn't start. The girl started screaming as the scratching sound got louder and closer to her door. Finally, the car started and he drove away. But then something started rattling outside the car door, so he put the pedal to the floor and drove a hundred miles an hour back to town. When they made it to her house, they got out of the car and there—hanging from the car's door handle—was a rusty hook!"

Mandy squealed and buried her face into Levi's chest. Levi grinned and nodded once at Connor. Lydia sat up straight and pressed a palm against her middle. "Connor, that was a terrible story!"

He beamed. "It scared you, didn't it?"

"Yes." She gave him a sour look and he snickered.

Mandy leaned forward and pointed at Bethany. "Connor, look what you've done: Bethany is scared silent."

"No, I'm not." Bethany imagined the couple's date, a man with a missing hand who was now missing his hook, and the inscrutable details of life outside the Land. She looked at Connor. "So what happened next? Did the man get his hook back?"

Connor laughed, but he gave no reply. Mandy covered her mouth with four thin fingers while she giggled at Bethany's question. Levi groaned. "That isn't the point, Beth."

Bethany sensed their arcane knowledge made the story more entertaining for them than for her. She glanced at their faces and grinned— not out of delight but out of embarrassment. "So what is the point?"

Her bewilderment amused her siblings and their spouses. While their laughter rang above the sound of the waves, she looked at Everett. He did not laugh with them but simply tilted his head toward her. "Don't worry about it, Beth," he whispered as he gave her side a soft nudge. She nudged him back and returned her gaze to the fire.

* * *

The dawn's light gave the grassless pottery yard a pink tint, making Bethany hopeful the morning would warm quickly. She carefully closed the tricky latch on the pottery yard's gate to avoid pinching her fingers. Mrs. Vestal lumbered out of the thatch-roofed shelter. "The clay is too cold this morning."

"Good morning," Bethany greeted her mentor as she stepped into the shelter and reached for a balled-up apron from the disorganized bench behind her pottery wheel. "It seems too soon for autumn weather."

"Only a week left until the equinox." Mrs. Vestal gave a grunt and bent to pick a stray shard from the dirt. She dropped the shard into a bucket of broken pottery pieces. Then she straightened her spine and rubbed her low back. "A boy from your class came by and asked about you after you left yesterday."

"Who was it?"

"One of the McIntosh boys—Phoebe's cousin, I think. My eyes aren't what they used to be, and boys change into men so quickly at your age."

Bethany shook out the crusty apron. "It doesn't seem that quick to me."

"He yelled over the gate and asked me if I knew who you wanted to court when you turned eighteen." Mrs. Vestal scratched her scalp, making the thick bun on top of her head wobble. "Asked me—as if I would know your plans."

"If I did want to court anyone, you would know."

"And if I knew anything of the sort, I certainly wouldn't have told him—let alone yelled it out to the street." Mrs. Vestal took a few arthritic steps into the shelter. "He didn't seem nice enough for you. You're a Colburn and there are not many men who live up to Colburn standards."

Bethany thought of her father and Levi and Connor—even though Connor was not a Colburn—and agreed with Mrs. Vestal. She tied on her apron. "I can't think of one boy from my class that I would even consider marrying."

"Well, he seemed keen on asking to court you."

"That makes two of them."

"Who is the other?" Mrs. Vestal raised an eyebrow. "Everett Foster?"

Bethany was confounded by the mention of Everett wanting to court her. A villager walked past the pottery yard, so she lowered her voice. "No, someone Phoebe mentioned to me yesterday. Besides, I don't think Everett feels that way about me."

"If you don't want to court, tell your father and he will send the boys away." Mrs. Vestal trudged to the meticulous shelves near her pottery wheel at the back of the shelter. "You're not like your siblings. Well—that's not entirely true—Lydia didn't want to marry either until Connor came along. And it's a wonder your brother got Mandy to marry him. I think that girl let every man from here to Southpoint court her. When you meet the right man, you will finally feel intrigue like all the other girls your age."

"Most of the girls my age are either already married or about to be." Bethany sighed. "And I have no problem with intrigue—I like falling in love—but I don't like everyone watching me to see what I will decide. And it seems like there are so many rules." She brushed the dried clay flecks from her apron. "I've heard Connor tell Lydia about the differences in our culture and the outside world, and it seems like we have restrictions other people don't have to worry about. And Father always expects so many things from me that the other girls in the village don't have to do."

Mrs. Vestal waved a hand. "You're nervous that's all; it's your age. The traditions are wise, and so are your father's edicts. Imagine if he allowed his daughters to court earlier than eighteen. You couldn't have dealt with all this while finishing school and an apprenticeship. Don't worry about what the other girls in the village are doing—or the outside world, for that matter. You don't have the wherewithal to focus on too many things at once and that's fine—I was the same way and it never hurt me. I live a perfectly pleasant life."

"Yes, well, since I finally finished school like Father said to, I can focus on the one thing I actually want to do." Bethany picked up a stack of work orders.

"See there, his plans were good for you. If you hadn't finished your schooling, you wouldn't have known how to use the materials found in that space debris last year." Mrs. Vestal pointed across the pottery yard at a small brick building. "I can fire that kiln hundreds of degrees hotter with that salvaged insulation and now we make ceramic that is nearly unbreakable. That's what half of those work orders are for—your ceramic, especially the relief glaze designs."

Bethany glanced at the orders. "They all want black pigment. I need more potash." As she flipped through the grayish slips of paper, she thought of the old airplane below the bluffs. She did not want to go back there. She almost asked where else she could find the minerals she needed, but then glanced at Mrs. Vestal and noticed her pained expression.

Bethany motioned with the work orders. "I can handle all of these. Why don't you go home and lie down."

"I believe I will." Mrs. Vestal nodded. "If you're sure."

"Of course." Bethany laid the stack of paper on her shelf and dropped a chunk of feldspar atop it to keep the pages from blowing away. Then she lifted the bucket of broken shards and dumped them into a grinder to make grog while she waited for the sun to heat the clay.

\* \* \*

By noon, Bethany's shadow was short and close to her feet as she walked away from the shelter that housed the pottery wheels. She squatted near a board propped across two wooden blocks on the ground and inspected the earthenware clay that was warming in the sun. Her hands instinctively knew when the clay was ready to use. She selected a tepid lump and knelt on the earth while she wedged the clay repeatedly on the board, working out the bubbles. It was still cooler than she preferred, but it would have to do.

Bethany rose and continued to work the clay with both hands as she carried it back to her pottery wheel. She sat at the wheel and positioned one foot on the ground and one foot over the concrete flywheel ready to kick it into motion. Wetting a sponge to dampen her pottery wheel, she gently kicked the flywheel rhythmically and dropped the lump of clay onto the center of the wheel head's turning surface. As she sank her thumbs into the spinning clump's warm, pliable middle, Bethany's creative verve tempted her to experiment. She quelled her enthusiasm and began to make the first of a six-bowl order.

The clay's shape changed with each slight movement of her hands. She slowly lifted and spread it as it spun around on the wheel and expanded into a smooth, thick cylinder. She reached her clay-covered fingers to a pot of milky water. Gathering a few droplets at a time, she sprinkled the clay to keep it moist as she molded it. Pleased with the bowl's final shape, she slipped her potter's knife along the base of the slowly spinning bowl and carved a groove around the bottom. Finally, she inserted a clean needle tool into the groove and cut the bowl away from the wheel head.

Believing she was alone, Bethany jumped when she saw Everett standing at the edge of the pottery shelter. She managed to hang onto the wet bowl despite the startle. Bethany laughed at herself then turned to the workbench behind her wheel and placed the bowl on its cluttered surface. As she turned back to her wheel, she glanced at Everett. He leaned his shoulder casually against the shelter's corner post as he watched her work. She looked down at her clay-splattered arms and felt a wave of self-consciousness. "Have you been standing there long?"

"No, not long." Everett grinned as he stuffed his hands in his pockets. He snapped his head to the side, tossing his hair off his forehead. "You seemed so focused on that clay. I didn't want to disrupt your concentration. What are you working on?"

"Trade orders. Bowls mostly." Bethany brushed the drying clay from her fingertips and walked into the sunshine to select another warm lump of clay. She knelt and worked the clay on the board for a moment, and then carried it back into the shelter.

Everett motioned to the other pottery wheel. "Is Mrs. Vestal here today?"

"She went home." Bethany sat at her wheel and, with a soft kick, set the flywheel into motion. Then she smirked. "Why? Have you come to place an order?"

"No." Everett chuckled and stepped forward. He drew his hands from his pockets and reached them up to the crossbeam of the shelter mere inches over his head. "Only you could make me smile on a day like today, Beth."

"Oh? What has made today so bad?" She watched his face while she pressed the clay in her hands. When his smile quickly faded, she felt his sadness, though it was rarely concealed of late. "Is you father's illness getting worse?"

Everett dropped his arms to his sides and blew out a breath. "He's only conscious a few minutes at a time. He hasn't eaten in three days. Mother believes his time has come." His voice broke and he looked away.

Bethany sensed his grief and her heart felt heavy as she shaped the clay. She pulled back from the spinning lump. If she were not covered in the watery dirt, she would have embraced Everett, held him, told him to weep if he wanted to, even though she knew he wouldn't. She followed his line of vision to the road in front of the pottery yard and saw people walking by. He would not express his grief with other people around. She whispered, "I'm so sorry for you, Everett… and for Mandy and your mother. Is there anything Lydia can do for your father to make him better?"

"No. She's made him comfortable. That's all she can do."

"The gray leaf medicine doesn't help?"

"No."

"Why not?"

"My father's heart has been defective since birth. When he was born, Doctor Ashton said he wouldn't live to adulthood. Father proved him wrong, but the gray leaf does nothing for this type of ailment—it only heals infections and wounds."

"That doesn't seem fair. He should be working his farm and enjoying life, not dying, especially since we have the medicine of the gray leaf tree. How can it cure infection and rapidly heal injuries but not stop a disease a person was born with?" When Everett did not answer, Bethany wiped the back of her hand across her forehead. "Is there anything I can do?"

Everett shook his head. "You're sweet, Beth. I hope you know that. You're truly good."

His approval encouraged her. "Should I tell my father to cancel my party?"

"No. In fact, that's why I came. My mother sent me to relay her regrets—she won't be attending tomorrow evening. She's afraid to leave his side. She wants to be with him when he passes."

"I understand. And if you decide to stay home with them, I will understand that too."

"No, my mother insists I go." He grinned slightly. "She knows I have been looking forward to your eighteenth birthday for a long time."

"As have I—though it's feeling less joyous as it approaches."

"Because of my father's condition?"

"No."

"Why then?"

If she could tell anyone how she truly felt, it was Everett. She stared at her hands as she continued working the spinning clay. "I have daydreamed about turning eighteen for years. I watched my sisters and brother all grow up and get to do what they wanted and I wanted that too. There were times when I thought I might burst if I had to wait another day to be finished with school and… be allowed to court. But now that I have only one day left, I'm dreading my birthday. Not because of the work—I love my work. It's the rest of it… the courting and the expectations of our traditions."

Everett crossed his arms over his chest, and the motion caught Bethany's eye. She glanced up at him then dampened the clay and finished shaping the bowl. "It wouldn't worry me except that when anyone mentions my birthday, they also mention courting. Apparently, every person in the village knows my father's rule about his daughters. I hate feeling like people are watching my decisions. I've been told about two different boys who are planning to ask my father's permission to court me and—"

"Who?" Everett spit the word forcefully, surprising Bethany.

"It doesn't matter who. The point is: I don't know if I want to be courted yet."

"Tell your father to send them away."

"Mrs. Vestal said the same thing."

Everett lifted a palm. "Then why not do it?"

"Because I want to have… possibilities." She glanced at him as she said it and was puzzled by his expression. His green eyes were intent and piercing like she had said something vulgar. She did not like the feeling of disappointing him and looked away. "Never mind, I can't explain it."

"Explain what? You want men to court you but not with the purpose to marry."

"No." Bethany flinched enough to cause a slight sway in the incomplete bowl as it whirled around on the wheel. She recovered in time to reshape it and, as she did, she felt Everett's eyes waiting expectantly for her defense. "That's not my desire at all. I simply want the freedom to court but not with all the pressure. Most of the girls my age are already married. Phoebe is my only unmarried friend and she is soon-to-be engaged to a man who has courted her only three weeks. Sometimes I just feel like our traditions are too—"

"So you plan to accept suitors and enjoy their attention then refuse them when they propose marriage?"

"No, I—"

"Ask Mandy what emptiness that hobby brought her. My sister will happily advise against that game."

"I have no desire to play games with any man's affection, Everett. I only meant that... oh, never mind." Bethany cut the completed bowl from the wheel. She turned to search for a bare spot on the workbench but found none. Everett moved behind her and cleared a space without her asking. "Thank you," she mumbled as she watched him rearrange the contents of the workbench to create space for her.

He brushed his hands together and stepped back. "Just enjoy the party your family gives you tomorrow and don't think of what else may come. This party is all Mandy has talked about for days, and your sisters are probably excited too."

Bethany smiled at Everett, realizing he was trying to cheer her up. She stood from her wheel and wiped her hands on her apron. As she thought of Samuel's condition, she regretted mentioning her petty troubles. "You're right. And I'm glad you will be there."

Everett scooted the dirt on the ground with the edge of his boot. "I want you to be happy, Beth. And that's why I think you should tell your father to send the scamps away." He grinned, giving her instant relief.

"I know I can always trust you to watch out for me." She stepped around him and into the sunny yard to gather another warm lump of clay. Then she chuckled. "Between your protectiveness and Levi's, it would be a miracle if any man were daring enough to ask me to court anyway."

# Chapter Two

Justin Mercer unscrewed the lid from the top of a vitamin supplement bottle. He sprinkled two of the soil-smelling capsules into his cupped hand. After popping the pills into his open mouth, he held them under his tongue and reached for a glass of water. As he swallowed, he noticed the expiration date printed on the label. Though alone in his cabin, he shrugged. One could not expect fresh supplements on a stolen ship adrift in the middle of the South Atlantic Ocean during a world war.

Mercer tipped the glass high and drank the rest of the water then shivered at its aftertaste. Though Volt had said the ship's fresh water generator was self-maintaining, Mercer was certain such putrid-tasting water was not healthy. He set the glass on the table beside his bed.

The room was called the captain's cabin, but Mercer was no ship's captain. Volt had controlled most of the bridge operations during the past nine months at sea, but he was no captain either. He was the mastermind behind their theft of the ship and he had even become the closest friend that Mercer had known since the war began, but Volt was no captain. Mercer could not blame Volt for their failed mission. After nine months of crossing the ocean over and over at the coordinates where there should be land, they were still stuck on the purloined icebreaker. It was not Volt's fault. He had done everything Mercer suggested.

The coordinates were seared upon Mercer's mind. He was in the right place—beneath the sky where he and Lieutenant Connor Bradshaw had been ejected from their aircraft. The crash's three-year anniversary was on the equinox—less than a week away. He thought of the coming autumn and turned to look out the window above his bed. The afternoon sun reflected off the water in piercing rays that made him squint. Soon the days would be short and the sea air cold. With a contagious illness onboard, he would keep the windows open until the cold forced him to close them even though after nine months with the crew, he had probably been exposed already. The plague of antibiotic-resistant tuberculosis had decimated the Southern Hemisphere's population long before they took the ship and left the Falklands. Now five of the original ten men aboard were dead. The last burial at sea left them without an electrical engineer. Mercer had read and reread every technical manual onboard the mid-size nuclear-powered icebreaker and still had no idea why its engines were down to limited power. They had yet to encounter another vessel or see any aircraft, and after years of a destructive world war and the disease that followed, he doubted they would.

Feeling caged in his cabin, Mercer reached for a technical manual from the foot of his bed and left the room. He walked through the narrow corridor of the quiet ship, ascended a short flight of steps, and opened the teak-paneled door to the bridge. Volt was sitting in one of two plush leather chairs with his skinny legs crossed at the ankle. Mercer closed the door and dropped the heavy manual on the chart table. Volt didn't acknowledge the noise. From behind the high back of Volt's chair, Mercer assumed Volt was reading, but as he walked to the instrument panels, he glanced at Volt and saw his head was slumped atop his shoulder. Mercer decided to let him rest but then he noticed Volt's awkward position and took a step toward him, wondering if he should wake him. He stood near the chair, dithering for a moment, when Volt roused from his sleep and coughed raucously. Mercer stepped close to an open window to breathe the outside air.

"Sorry, mate. How long was I out?"

"I don't know. I just came up for the night shift." Mercer looked through the front windows of the bridge at the waning sunlight. "Any change in engine output?"

"I'm afraid not." Volt coughed again, this time into his elbow. "There is something I need to do, but I wanted to let you know first."

Mercer moved to the chair next to Volt and sat, expecting technical details of the ship's operation. "What is it?"

"I'm going to bring the Unified States satellite communications back online."

Mercer thought of his fellow officers in the Unified States Navy and the destruction the communication severance caused his country. Since the day he met Volt, he had presumed Volt's occupation in technical terrorism caused the communication shutdown for the Unified States, but he never expected Volt to admit it. The last strand of Mercer's frayed patriotism told him to be angry, but he looked at the man who had become his friend and felt only compunction for luring him into the middle of the ocean with the promise of a pristine land that apparently did not exist after all. Volt's health was failing. He would die on the ship like the other men, and Mercer felt it was his fault.

He rested his elbows on his knees and studied Volt's emaciated face. "Why now?"

Volt's fingers twined a length of string at a rip in the knee of his faded jeans. He shrugged his thin shoulders. "If there is anyone out there who can help you—I want you to be able to return to your people." He motioned to the door. "Our men are sick—all of them. I've got it bad, too. You're the only person aboard that's still healthy. I have the equipment in my cabin and the ship still has enough power. After I get communications back online, I'll send a message in your name, saying you caught me. I'll be dead before anyone gets here. You can tell them I took the ship while you were working on it. One scan of my DNA and they'll hail you a hero for turning in my dead body." Volt grinned but it didn't reach his eyes.

Mercer's throat tightened. He cleared it and looked away from Volt. "We don't even know if the Unified States still exists. If we send a signal, anyone could intercept it."

"The States will still exist in some form. You Yanks always rebuild; you're a tough lot."

Mercer looked back at him. "I shouldn't have brought you out here."

"Brought me?" Volt laughed then choked and coughed blood onto his sleeve. "I caught this disease before I ever heard of you, Lieutenant Justin Mercer, and your fantasy of an uncharted land. I would've died wherever I went. I'm glad I spent the last few months of my life searching for land out here away from the war. I got to have one last adventure and for that I'm grateful to you, mate. I'll not leave you stranded out here if I can help it." Volt began coughing again. When his breathing settled enough to speak, he looked up at Mercer. "Tell you what, mate, get me to my cabin and I'll start working on it now."

Mercer rose and reached out to help Volt up. Volt stood and his legs shook beneath him. He sat back down and sank into the chair, breathless. "On second thought, let me rest a moment, then get me to my cabin."

\* \* \*

Bethany lifted the last breakfast plate from the bottom of the sudsy water in the kitchen sink. She gave the plate a quick wash and set it in the crowded dish rack. As she began to wring out the cloth, Connor slid his dirty plate into the sink. "Hang on—one more," he said as he breezed past.

Bethany caught his eye as she swirled the cloth over the dirty dish in the soapy water. "Are you going to take care of the, um, thing below the bluffs?"

"No, I have a class to teach today." Connor glanced at the others seated at the kitchen table behind them. He furrowed his brow and lowered his voice. "Remember what we talked about, Beth. Prove I can trust you, okay?"

"Of course."

"Happy birthday," he called to her over his shoulder as he strode out the back door.

Bethany wanted to tell someone about the old plane and the remains of the pilot inside, but—more than that—she liked having a secret with

Connor. She turned to check the kitchen table for any more dishes before she drained the water. The dishes were cleared but her father and great-aunt remained seated at opposite ends of the otherwise empty table. Isabella was holding her cane close to her as if she wanted to get up but could not muster the energy.

John stood from the table and grinned at Bethany. "Adeline and Maggie should arrive from Woodland around noon."

"Are their families coming, too?" Isabella asked.

"Yes." John scowled at Isabella's question. Then his features returned to their usual pleasantness and he fixed his gaze on his daughter. "Bethany, they will expect you to stay out of the kitchen while they prepare for your party."

"Gladly. Besides, Lydia has already ordered me upstairs for the afternoon. Mandy is coming to give me curls." Bethany flipped her brown hair over her shoulder then opened an upper cabinet and drew a dishtowel from a stack on the shelf. Her father took the towel from her hand. He winked at her and began drying the dishes. "I know how you feel about housework, so I will spare you this one chore, but only because it is your birthday."

She kissed her father's bearded cheek. "Thank you."

He drew his head back a degree and looked at the top of her head. "Have you grown?"

"Goodness!" Isabella exclaimed, still seated at the table. She turned her head in their direction, but her unseeing eyes moved erratically. "How tall is she now, John?"

Bethany felt like a child as her father angled his head. He studied her while he dried a dish. "I would guess she is an inch under six foot. We will have to measure you later—against the trim in the parlor like your mother used to."

"Nearly six foot? You'd better not grow any more!" Isabella's lips moved between sentences. "What man will marry you if he cannot reach your lips to kiss you?"

Bethany groaned. She hated when people commented on her height as if she could control her own growth—and as if true love could be deterred by such a trivial factor. She gave a sideways glance to Isabella and grinned. "Actually, I have decided not to marry at all."

Isabella snickered. "No, dear, at best you have decided to put off marriage. I decided not to marry at all. You aren't restricted by any impairment other than your disdain for domestic responsibility. Oh, you will marry— just like your sisters and your brother did before you. Mark my words: you will marry too. And soon, I imagine, now that you are eighteen. I was surprised there were no men on the doorstep at sunrise this morning with flowers in hand."

Bethany leaned her hip against the countertop. "And if there were, I would have refused to answer the door."

"I have prayed for years that the good Lord would let me live long enough to see all five of you children find love," Isabella said. "You are the last one and I'm not getting any younger, so you had better get on with it, dear. You are grown now; it's time you were married to a good man—and apparently you will need a tall one. You might be the baby of the family, but you're not a child any longer."

Bethany looked at her father, hoping he would save her from Isabella's commentary. The dishes clanked as John stacked them into the cupboard. He glanced at Bethany and shrugged. "She is right—you are not a child anymore."

Hearing her father pronounce her adult status gave Bethany an uneasy feeling. She crossed her long arms over her body. "I'm not going to marry simply because my sisters did. Besides, I know all the boys in Good Springs, and there isn't one I would consider a good man."

Isabella stood and moved away from the table. "You probably won't find a man who compares to the example your father has set for you. A man had to drop out of the sky for Lydia to consider marriage." She chuckled as she tapped her cane in front of her and inched toward the parlor. "Maybe the Foster boy will take a romantic interest in you someday; he has the same spirit as your father, and I hear he has grown tall too."

Bethany turned to John and silently pretended to writhe in pain and scream. He beamed at her dramatic display then straightened his face. "Thank you, Aunt Isabella."

"Happy birthday, dear," Isabella murmured as she left the room.

Bethany wiped both hands over her face and heaved a sigh. Boys wanted to ask her to court, the village had certain expectations of her, and her great aunt was waiting for her to marry so she could die happy. Bethany leaned against the counter and looked at her father. "Do you think I need to marry? I don't—at least not anytime soon. I'm too young."

John shook his head. "You are not too young. You are not ready, but not too young. You have been well protected in this family, and that helps preserve your virtue in many ways. But your life is ahead of you, along with the experiences that will help you mature."

"So I'm not too young, but I'm too immature to marry?"

John closed the cupboard doors and draped the damp muslin towel over the empty dish rack. He let out a breath then leaned a palm on the countertop and looked at her. "Maturity—in the sense of complete emotional development—is not required for marriage. In fact, that kind of maturity takes years of adult life to develop. However, a person does need to be mature in that she has realistic expectations of life and responsibility and love." He held up a finger to emphasize a point. "What your friends call intrigue is not true love. The love that is needed for marriage is not simply good feelings, it is submitting to the needs of someone else. Real love requires sacrifice. Sacrifice requires self-denial, and that takes maturity. You are the youngest in the house and you have never had to take care of much around here, so I understand if the responsibility of managing a household frightens you. But it is not a matter of age—it is a matter of having realistic expectations."

Bethany studied her cuticles as her father spoke. When he gave advice, his tone of voice was similar to the tone he used every Sunday in the pulpit. Having been raised under the capable leadership of the village overseer, she was habituated to his wisdom. When he spoke at length, her thoughts immediately drifted. She thought of the airplane buried below the bluffs, her upcoming party, her work at the pottery yard, Everett, and then she thought of Everett's father, Samuel Foster, ill and soon to pass away. She wanted to see him one last time.

"Bethany?" John inclined his head, regaining her attention.

"Yes?"

"Do you understand then?"

"Yes, Father. Realistic expectations." She lifted her hands in resignation and stepped to the back door. "There's something I need to do."

"I thought Mrs. Vestal gave you the day off."

"She did."

"Bethany," John's parental tone stopped her as she walked to the door. "Do not go near that old airplane."

"You know about it?" She whirled around to face him.

"Of course. Connor told me. He and Levi are going down at low tide tomorrow to bury the pilot's remains and see what they can salvage from the plane, but no one else knows and that is how we want to keep it. Understand?"

"Yes, Father."

"So where are you going then?"

Bethany glanced back at her father before walking out the door. "I'm going to visit Mr. Foster."

* * *

Dried summer grass crunched beneath Everett's boots as he walked away from the lambing pens toward the barn. Though the pens would not be used again until lambing began in the early spring, Everett had taken the time to fix a gate, knowing the importance of keeping up with repairs around the sheep farm.

As he approached the barn, the wind shifted directions, delivering the scent of the winter grass that was already sprouting in the pastures. He considered the sweet aroma proof that the flock would be sustained by nature over the coming months. Two of his four herding dogs were pacing behind the barn; the other two were with the new shepherd, James, and the flock. The dogs were as anxious as Everett to move the sheep back from the western pastures. That was James' job now, but still Everett wanted to ride out and accompany him, since it would be his first time to drive the flock home. He planned to begin the two-day chore after Bethany's birthday party, which meant the drive would have to wait one more day.

Everett tossed open the side door of the expansive barn. He glanced back at the afternoon sun, gauging the hour before he stepped inside. When he shut the door, his vision blackened for a moment as his eyes adjusted to the dim light inside the barn. Nicholas Vestal, the newly hired farmhand, was in a stall doctoring a wounded calf. Everett leaned against the stall gate. "Is she all right?"

Nicholas rubbed gray leaf salve into the calf's hind leg. "I think so. This will remove the infection."

"She couldn't be in better hands."

"I hope you're right." Nicholas stuffed a piece of cloth into the top of the salve bottle. "I never thanked you properly for giving me work here. I want you to know I'm grateful for the chance to earn my own flock."

"You're welcome. You came highly recommended by your aunt and we're glad to have you. Is the shepherd's cabin adequate accommodation for you and James both?"

Nicholas nodded. "More than I could ask for."

"I'm glad to hear it."

The calf leaned into Nicholas' leg. He ran a hand across its back. "Any change in Mr. Foster's condition?"

"No." Everett removed his hat and stared at it while he mindlessly rubbed the brim between his fingers. "I'm going to the house now to get cleaned up. I'll let you know if anything changes before I leave."

"Oh, yes, the Colburn girl's birthday party is tonight." Nicholas grinned, swelling his wooly sideburns. "Some of the fellows mentioned it at the market Saturday."

"It's a private party."

"Right, well, they spoke fondly of Bethany."

Though Everett's aggression was not directed at Nicholas, the thought of men talking about Bethany rankled. He considered it a personal affront when any man expressed desire for her, no matter how subtle. "What fellows?"

Nicholas frowned. "A couple of boys who said they knew her from school, that's all."

"What did they say?"

"Something about courting her after her eighteenth birthday. It sounded like she has a lot of admirers."

"Admirers?" Everett knew every young man in Good Springs. He immediately began a mental list of his possible competition for Bethany's affection and his pulse quickened. "Who?"

Nicholas wiped his hands on his pants. "I'm not one of them, of course. She's a great girl, I'm sure. My Aunt Vestal speaks well of her, but she's not for me."

"No, she's not." Everett turned to leave but stopped when he noticed the calf licking the salve from its wounded leg. He pointed at the calf. "You'll need to wrap that leg." When Nicholas nodded and reached for bandaging material, Everett tapped his fist on the stall gate and walked away.

* * *

Bethany waited on the cushioned seat in front of her dressing table while Mandy and Lydia rifled through her wardrobe. She crossed her long legs under her body and traced her finger along the silver links of her favorite bracelet as she watched the women in the dressing table's mirror. They were scrutinizing every sartorial item she owned. She lifted a hand. "Why shouldn't I wear the black dress?"

"Because you are not in mourning," Lydia replied as she pulled a sky blue dress from the wardrobe and inspected its seams.

Mandy tossed an auburn curl over her shoulder and glanced at Lydia. "She likes the black dress because it makes her look older."

Bethany sighed, her patience waning. "No, I like the red dress because it makes me look older. I like the black dress because it was Mother's."

Mandy and Lydia exchanged a look and continued selecting an outfit for her party. She would have enjoyed being primped by either her sister or sister-in-law, but the two of them together were able to override Bethany's every opinion effortlessly.

Mandy picked up another dress, raised it high while she examined it, and then put it back. "The overseer's daughters never lack dresses, do they?"

"This from the woman whose husband just built her a second wardrobe." Lydia continued to finger the sky blue dress.

"The seamstress needed a nursery added to the Ashton house, so Levi bartered for a few dresses." Mandy winked at Bethany. "I can't help it if he dotes on me."

Lydia lifted the dress and its hem glided across the floor. "See if she has any gloves to go with this."

Mandy reached to Bethany's dresser, selected a pair of beige gloves, then held them close to the dress in Lydia's arms. Mandy tilted her head. "I guess these will do."

Lydia poked the gloves. "That one is stained."

"Do I have to wear gloves? They make my hands feel trapped." Bethany returned her eyes to the silver bracelet that was lying open on her dressing table. The delicate links clinked as she made them spiral around and around across the wooden tabletop. She touched the tiny charm that dangled from one link and thought back to when Levi gave her the bracelet. Her brother doted on her too, though somewhat less now that he had a wife.

Mandy returned to the dresser drawer and sifted through its contents. "All of your gloves have stains. Your days of playing in the dirt must end, or you will never have a decent wardrobe."

"I'm a potter." Bethany rolled her eyes. "I'm not afraid of dirt."

Lydia stepped around the bed and unbuttoned the dress, removing it from its padded hanger.

"Well tonight your entry to adulthood will be celebrated, and a woman should know how to behave in her best clothes and keep them clean." She smiled at Bethany. "You may borrow my dress gloves. Try to stay out of the dirt."

Mandy sauntered to the dressing table. "I remember being eighteen—the dreaming, the innocence—"

"Innocence? Ha!" Lydia snorted. "Ignorance is more like it. Just because we didn't know what we were doing does not mean we were innocent."

"The intrigue, the flirting." Mandy grinned in the mirror then lifted a comb to Bethany's wavy, brown hair. "And the freedom to make your own choices. I remember walking to the beach every day simply because I didn't have to go to school anymore. I could work when I wanted, for as long as I wanted, and then walk to the village on a whim. Of course, most of my friends were married within a year after leaving school and soon had babies. Enjoy the freedom while you have it, Bethany."

Lydia shook the dress open and fluffed the skirt. "I was halfway through my medical training at eighteen. In fact, I helped deliver a baby on my eighteenth birthday. Freedom indeed—for my patient anyway."

Bethany listened to Lydia and Mandy reminisce. Though they spoke wistfully of their new adult years, she thought it must feel better to be their age—secure in their skin, able to make their homes, and confident in their love for devoted husbands. She imagined herself, twenty-five and confident, fussing over a younger woman and speaking of life from experience.

"Bethany." Lydia motioned for her to stand.

Bethany unfurled her legs from the cushioned seat and stood. She felt like a doll as they dressed her. Lydia situated the soft fabric at the front of the dress while Mandy fastened the score of tiny pearl buttons up her spine. She looked down at her pigment-stained cuticles then hid her fingertips in her fists, hoping Lydia would not notice. The women tightened the dress around her boyish waist while commenting on her height. The year-old dress had been made to skim the floor, but now it hovered well above her ankles. She glanced down at her boney shins. "It's just as well since the party is outdoors. Maybe I won't stain the hem."

"That's the spirit!" Mandy beamed. "And I'll give your hair such pretty ringlets no one will look at your ankles. Now sit back down so I can reach your head."

"Very funny," Bethany said, sarcastically.

Mandy began pinning Bethany's hair into sections while Lydia busied herself with the discarded clothing, smoothing each garment as she put it away. Bethany did not have to look to know that her sister was also arranging the contents of her wardrobe in some logical order. Lydia stopped organizing when the sounds of Andrew waking from his nap drifted down the hallway. Bethany glanced at Lydia in the mirror as she disappeared toward the nursery.

Mandy drew a section of Bethany's hair through her thin fingers then spun it and pinned it close to her scalp. Bethany watched Mandy in the mirror and studied her perfect features, wishing they were her own. Mandy's face was lean, her nose sloped up at the end, and her chin came to a proud point. Bethany looked at her own reflection in the mirror and decided her dimples looked childish, her cheeks were too pink, and her puffy lips seemed fixed in a sulky pout even when she was not sulking. Though she disparaged most of her features comparatively, she appreciated the blue of her eyes because everyone said they were exactly like her father's. She glanced at Mandy's green eyes and wondered if Mandy and Levi's children would have Mandy's green eyes or Levi's golden brown. Baby Andrew resembled Connor; maybe all boy babies resembled their fathers. As Bethany gazed at Mandy in the mirror, she wondered what it felt like to be the beauty of the village, captivating men instead of intriguing boys.

Mandy began to unpin and arrange the loose curls she had formed in Bethany's hair, the length of which now barely skimmed her collarbones. She lifted the hair on one side and clipped it high with an embellished silver hairpin, exposing Bethany's ear.

Mandy leaned down and looked at her in the mirror. "What do you think of that?"

Bethany lifted her chin admiring Mandy's work. She looked less childish than she had mere moments before. In her estimation, Mandy improved everything she touched. "Beautiful."

Mandy gave Bethany's shoulders a squeeze. "You certainly are."

"Thank you."

"Wait until the boys see you."

"As long as I make it through the evening without any boys proposing, I will be pleased." She made a face at the thought of courting the former classmates who were rumored to be planning to ask her father's permission.

"Perhaps not boys then." Mandy inclined her head. "Are there any men who have a chance at your heart?"

Bethany shook her head. "The only men I know are either married or are my relatives."

"What about Everett?"

"Everett is my friend—my best friend."

"What about Nicholas, the new farmhand?

"Mrs. Vestal's nephew?"

"Yes. He's handsome enough, don't you think?"

"I don't want to think about courting." She lowered her voice as the bedroom door opened. Dismissing Mandy's question, Bethany reached for the bracelet on the dressing table. She laid her wrist across it and clasped its ends together.

Lydia walked into the room holding her baby. She smiled at Bethany. "Oh, little sister, you look beautiful!"

There was something about the way Lydia looked when she said it that reminded Bethany of her mother. Though Bethany did not trust her memories of her mother's face, she studied Lydia's eyes for a moment, but then felt an abysmal ache and had to look away.

* * *

Everett passed a comb through his clean wet hair before he buttoned the cuffs at his wrists and left his bedroom. As he walked through the hallway, he glanced into his parents' room. His father was awake; his mother was sitting in a chair beside the bed. Everett stopped and tapped a knuckle against the doorframe.

Samuel lifted his head from the pillow. "Come in, son." The room had an acerbic scent that intensified each day as his father drew closer to death.

A small smile curved Roseanna's lips as she stood. "My, don't you look dashing!" She began straightening Everett's cravat and glanced back at Samuel. "Doesn't he look handsome?"

Everett did not mind her motherly attention, but he wanted to see his father while he had the chance. He craned his neck around his mother. "How are you feeling, Father?"

"Oh, I'm fine, son, just fine." Samuel wheezed out a breath. "Roseanna, let the boy alone so we can speak." She nodded then skirted Everett and left the room. Samuel motioned to the empty chair. "Have a seat. There are some things I want to say to you while there is still time."

Everett sensed his father was about to impart his final wishes and felt his throat tighten. He lowered himself into the chair. It was still warm. "I can stay home tonight if you wish."

"No, no. You should go to Bethany's party." Samuel smiled and his cheeks rounded. "She's a sweet girl—came to visit me today, you know."

"No, I didn't know."

"She did. Precious girl. She cried when she said goodbye." Samuel took a few shallow breaths. "John Colburn is a blessed man to have her for a daughter. She'll make an excellent wife for you one day."

Everett chuckled at his father's bluntness, but the sound was muffled by fluid emotion as he blinked back tears. Samuel lay quietly for a moment. While Everett waited for him to regain the strength to speak again, the stillness in the room pained him. He heard his mother busying herself in the kitchen. The clank of a kettle on the stove echoed down the hallway.

Samuel drew a quick breath. "How are the animals?"

"Excellent. Tomorrow I'll ride to the western pastures and help drive the flock home."

"And your new man—Nicholas—will he work out?"

"Yes, I believe so. He's a strong worker and good with the animals. He and James work well together."

"I'm glad to hear it." Samuel nodded as much as the pillow allowed. He seemed to gain a burst of strength. "I want you to hire men when you need them. You already manage the farm well and the flock has doubled under your care. You will no doubt see it prosper many times over. Never try to do it all yourself—hire men when you need them. And never let a needy man go without work. Our family has run this farm for six generations and we've never let a neighbor go hungry. Understand?"

"Yes, Father."

"Be fair with the men you hire so they prosper too. Never use your position to mistreat people. Take care of your mother for me. She may live another thirty years, and she likes to keep busy. Let her work all she wants."

"Yes, Father."

"And if something happens to Levi, you must take care of Mandy. I know John would take her in, but she's your sister. Promise me you will make sure she is taken care of."

"I promise."

"Marry young so you can raise children while you still have the energy."

"I can't promise you that."

"No, I reckon you can't." Samuel paused and looked up at the ceiling for a moment. "It meant so much that Bethany came to see me this afternoon. She's always been a special girl. She laughs when someone laughs and cries when he cries. Hannah had that same ability to commiserate. That's where Bethany got her sensitivity—from her mother. She sees life as a gift and that makes her look for the possibilities in every situation. I know you are fond of her, son."

"I am."

"She won't be available long now that she has reached the age that John lets his girls court. Speak to John. He will give you his blessing."

Everett nodded but said nothing. He wanted to tell his father that he had planned to court Bethany, but she said she wasn't ready. She needed time and he loved her enough to give her whatever she needed. He wanted to tell his father all of it, but Samuel's strength was already beginning to diminish. Samuel blinked several times, each time slower than the time before. At last his eyes remained closed. Everett leaned close and listened to his father's chest. He was still alive, just lost again in the unconscious depths that recurrently swallowed him for unpredictable expanses of time.

As Everett left home, his favorite dog hobbled to meet him in the yard. "Hello, old Shep." The dog lumbered beside Everett as he walked across the yard to the road. He stooped to pat the dog's head before leaving the property. Shep dropped his aged body to the ground as Everett walked away.

The mile walk on the road that led into the village of Good Springs put a needed distance between Everett and the farm he was soon to inherit. He stuffed his hands in his pockets as he walked along the gravel path and wondered if he had spoken to his father for the last time.

As he got close to the Colburn property at the southern edge of the village, he saw Connor and Levi lighting torches staked in the ground in front of the main house. John stood at the back door passing chairs out to two of his sons-in-law, while Bethany's eldest sisters arranged platters stacked high with food on a long table. One of Mandy's music students, backlit by the setting sun, stood near the medical cottage tuning her violin. Lydia stepped out of the house holding her baby in one arm and guiding their elderly aunt with the other. Phoebe McIntosh was whispering in the ear of a man who stood near a freshly lit torch. Everett assumed he was the man that Bethany had mentioned was soon to propose to Phoebe. He noticed two other young women from Bethany's class but no other men. Maybe John Colburn had already refused the competition, or maybe they had yet to arrive.

Everett stepped off the path from the road and onto the lawn in front of the Colburn house. After Levi lit the last torch, he pinched the match head, extinguishing its flame, and lifted his chin acknowledging Everett.

Everett removed his hands from his pockets and rubbed them together. "Need help with anything?"

Levi shook his head. "We're just waiting for Beth."

"Where is she?"

"Still inside with Mandy." Levi crossed his arms. "How's Samuel?"

"He was awake for a while this afternoon." Everett glanced at the house then at Bethany's family and friends moving about the yard. "Are you expecting anyone else tonight?"

"I hope not." Levi grinned.

"Did anyone come to talk to John about her today?"

"Not that I know of."

"Good."

"Are you still going to speak to him tonight?"

"I planned to, but yesterday she complained about boys wanting to ask her to court. She said she isn't ready for it. I think she was just nervous about her birthday, but I'm going to let it pass before I say anything." He noticed the crowd's sudden stillness. Heads began to turn in the direction of the Colburn house. Bethany stepped across the threshold and into the yard. Everett's senses instantly sharpened. He smelled the briny air that floated inland from the nearby ocean and heard the wind rustle through the gray leaf trees. His pulse thumped beneath his collar, but all he could see was Bethany. She smiled at the crowd. Dimples pitted her pink cheeks, and Everett took a step forward. Her friends thronged around her and admired her dress and her brown ringlets. He wished he could touch her hair and shoved his hands back into his pockets. She towered above the other girls, which made it easy for him to watch her face as she giggled with her friends. When he looked at her, everything changed for him. His troubled thoughts of work and family melted away. She glanced over her friends and met his gaze. When she smiled at

him, the air changed and he wondered if she
knew.

# Chapter Three

Justin Mercer wiped the mirror with his towel. When it immediately steamed back over, he wrapped his towel around his waist and opened the bathroom door. As the steam escaped the bathroom, he looked back at himself in the clearing mirror. The telltale redness in his cheeks confirmed the drops on his face were sweat from the fever, not steam from the shower. His energy felt as depleted as the ship's engines. He rarely got sick and loathed the feeling of oncoming illness.

Mercer leaned both palms on the edge of the sink and inspected his reflection. The fever's grip distorted his perception, revealing a stranger—a feverish wayfarer with shaggy hair. He wanted to see the confident naval flight officer who—before the war—could leave a bar with any woman he wanted. He stared at the wings of the insignia tattooed on his chest.

Becoming overwhelmed with the urge to look the part again, he reached for an electric clipper. Chunks of damp, black hair dropped into the sink with each pass of the clipper until all that remained was the buzz of a professional warrior.

Mercer began to step out of the bathroom then stopped when his vision blurred. He gripped the wall. After several deep breaths, he moved slowly into his cabin. He pulled on a pair of jeans and a worn-out t-shirt, then a sudden chill prompted him to put on the hooded sweatshirt he had owned since college. He sat on the edge of his bed shivering for a moment, then lay back and closed his eyes. This strain of tuberculosis had already killed half the crew. Only he and Volt and three other crewmen were still alive. The icebreaker's engines were down to limited power, leaving them adrift in the South Atlantic Ocean at the coordinates where Mercer's parachute had carried him three years before. He propped himself on his elbows and looked out the open window at the endless blue of ocean and sky. He should accept the fact that the land he saw during his emergency parachute's descent three years before simply did not exist, but the vivid memory would not fade. He had watched Lieutenant Connor Bradshaw's parachute drift toward a pristine shoreline while he was being carried out to sea. Replaying the memory brought a surge of fresh energy and quickened his sluggish heartbeat.

Mercer stood up and marched out of his cabin. He had come this far, and he was not going to die on the ship like the others. His hand grazed the laminate wall of the narrow corridor as he walked from his cabin to Volt's. He halted in front of Volt's door and lifted his hand to knock. When there was no answer, he let himself in the room.

Volt was sitting up in bed, his thin legs buried under the blankets. He had bulky black headphones covering his ears, a computer keyboard on his lap, and several touchscreen devices strewn beside him on the bed. He nodded at Mercer and held up a finger then looked back at his computer screen. Faint sounds came from Volt's headphones. His fingertips rapidly tapped the keys. Though he no longer had the strength to get out of bed, he was working tirelessly to restore the communications network he had once sabotaged.

Mercer closed the door then picked up a side chair and set it near Volt's bed. As he sat in the chair, Volt glanced at him and pointed at his hair then smiled. Mercer rubbed the top of his freshly buzzed head. Volt looked back at his screen as he typed with alacrity. His skin sagged from loss of hydration and his face bore the sallowness reserved for the terminal. He wheezed as he tapped a screen then removed his headphones. He slipped them down from his ears and let them wrap around the base of his whiskered neck. "It is working, mate. I'm starting to hear chatter out there. As soon as I can confirm these are Unified States allies on the network, I'll send our coordinates."

"That's great." As Mercer said the words, he knew he should feel relieved, but instead he felt a sudden sense of panic. He was so close to that land. He glanced out the porthole behind Volt's bed; that land was right here and he knew it. He could not stay and die on the ship waiting for a rescue. His chest tightened as his fingers tingled and his vision narrowed. "I'm leaving. I'm sorry, man, but I have to try."

"Try what, mate?"

"I'm sorry. I can't stay here—onboard. I'm coming down with the fever and I can't stay here and die. Not on this ship. I can't do it. The others can help keep things going until the rescue arrives, but I have to go."

Volt lifted a palm. "Go where?"

Mercer felt a headache coming on and his ears began to ring. "I'm taking a dinghy onto the water."

"Now?"

"Yes, now. The land is here. It's close. I just know it. Tomorrow is the third anniversary of the date I saw it—the date I floated on that water. Bradshaw made it to that land and I missed out somehow. I'm sick now and I will die soon, but I'm going to die trying. I have to.

I'm sorry, Volt. You have been the best friend I've had in years and I will never forget you." Mercer stood and backed toward the door. He studied Volt's face, believing it would be the last time he would ever see him.

Volt nodded and pressed his lips together. "Justin?"

"Yeah."

"Good luck, mate."

Mercer walked out of Volt's cabin and left the door open so the other men could hear if Volt needed them. He staggered through the corridor, up a short flight of stairs, and onto the deck.

The calm sea breeze cooled his face as he worked to untie the ropes that were holding an inflatable dinghy to the deck near the rail. He felt the thorny grip of the illness inside his chest. Knowing his volition could only empower his weakened body for so long, he forced himself to keep going. After checking that the outboard engine was secured to the transom plate, he lifted the dinghy over the railing and lowered it to the water below.

He coughed as he held the line linking the dinghy to the ship. He climbed over the railing and down an escape ladder then sat on the narrow seat of the dinghy. The ringing in his ears amplified as he removed a latch from the forward bridle and released the boat from the ship.

Gripping an oar in one hand, he reached the other hand around to the back of his empty waistband. It was foolish to leave the ship without his sidearm, but he was not going back now. He started the outboard motor and aimed the boat in the direction of the lowering sun.

\* \* \*

Bethany steadied a tall stack of clay bowls beneath her chin as she carried them out of the kiln. She set the stack on a worktable in the pottery shed, then she spread the bowls across the table to allow them to cool. Untying her apron, she stepped to a sink in the corner of the shelter and began to scrub her dirt-caked hands. As she picked at the clay beneath her fingernails, Mrs. Vestal hobbled to her pottery wheel in the opposite corner of the shelter.

"Are you done for the afternoon, Bethany?"

"If that's all right with you."

"Yes, that's fine." Mrs. Vestal did not look up from her clay when she spoke.

Bethany blew a stray strand of hair out of her eyes. "See you tomorrow then."

After Mrs. Vestal grunted a reply, Bethany nodded and wiped her wet hands on her skirt. She walked out of the shelter, crossed the pottery yard, and opened the wooden gate. As she closed it, the latch pinched her finger. A short gasp reflexively escaped her throat and she shook the sting out of her hand. Once the pain subsided, she examined her finger while she walked along the cobblestone street toward her family's home.

As she passed the sandy path that led through the forest from the beach, someone on the path caught her eye. She looked away from her red finger and saw a stranger walking out of the gray leaf forest and into the village. The memory of once being attacked by a stranger flashed through her mind. Her heart began to race and she scanned the village for anyone who could protect her. When she looked back at the man, Bethany noticed his clothing and was reminded of what Connor wore when he first arrived in the Land. Her fear began to dissipate and astonishment took its place. His gray shirt had block letters on the front that read: NAVY and his short haircut resembled Connor's old military style. He had to be from Connor's nation.

The man coughed and held a hand to his chest. His steps slowed to a near stagger as if he were ill or injured. Then his eyes met hers and surprise lit his face.

Bethany took several cautious steps toward him. "Are you all right?"

He stopped walking and his dark eyes widened. "You speak English!"

"Who are you? Where did you come from?" Bethany glanced around her as she stepped closer. "You look ill. Do you need help?"

He erected his posture and cast his gaze toward the buildings and houses in the village behind her. "What is this place?"

Bethany looked too, and then turned back to the stranger. "This is the village of Good Springs." She remembered what Connor had said about the Land being hidden from the outside world. "Oh, do you mean the Land?"

"The Land?" He raised an eyebrow.

"Yes. This place—we call it the Land."

After a short chuckle, he nodded. "That's fitting."

She wondered if he had parachuted to the Land like Connor did. She looked at the trees behind him and did not see any equipment. "How did you get here?"

The man coughed but did not answer her. She was almost certain he was one of Connor's people. Her curiosity had never been piqued with such vigor. Connor was brilliant and courteous and strong and now another man like him had arrived, and Bethany found him first. She felt like she had stumbled upon a great treasure and stepped within arm's reach of the man. "Are you from America? You sound just like Connor."

When she said Connor's name, he drew a quick breath and grabbed her arm. His hand was warm. "Connor Bradshaw? Lieutenant Bradshaw? Is he here? Do you know him?"

"Yes. Did you come here to find Connor?"

"I knew he was here." He took his hand off Bethany and ran his fingers over his short hair. A smile spread across his face. "I knew it. I just knew it."

His astonishment delighted her. "Connor is teaching at the school right now, but he should be finished soon. What's your name?"

"Mercer. Lieutenant Justin Mercer."

Her stomach tingled. "So you are a soldier?"

"No. I'm a naval flight officer—well, I used to be." He wiped the palm of his hand across his chest.

"In an army?"

"Navy."

"Oh, the Royal Navy?" she asked thinking of what Connor said about the old plane below the bluffs.

"No, Unified States. Have you had contact with the Royal Navy?"

"No." Bethany was not sure how his people addressed one another. She angled her head. "What shall I call you?"

"Justin." He grinned and held her gaze.

"All right, Justin… are you from Connor's nation?"

"Yes. And what shall I call you?"

"Bethany."

He lowered his chin. "Do you have a last name, Bethany?"

"Yes, it's Colburn." She looked at his mouth. "You speak like Connor. How did you get here?"

Again, no answer. He coughed into his sleeve. "Do you know Connor well?"

"He is my brother-in-law. You sound ill. Do you need to see the doctor?"

"You have doctors here?" He chuckled then nodded. "Yeah, I guess I do."

"I can show you to the medical cottage. It's just down the road." She motioned to her family's property. "My sister is the doctor in our village. Her name is Lydia, but you should call her Doctor Bradshaw."

Justin gave a short laugh as he began walking beside her. He seemed to have recouped some of his energy. "Doctor Bradshaw—as in Lieutenant Bradshaw's wife? He married the village's doctor? Why that lucky—"

When Bethany glanced at him, he cut his words short. She looked back at the path to the shore as they stepped onto the road. "Did you come here alone?"

"Yeah."

"From America?"

"No, I have been on a ship for the past few months."

"With your navy?"

"No, another ship."

"Where is your ship now?"

"It's still out there." He pointed his thumb toward the ocean. "Is this an American settlement?"

She glanced in the direction of the ocean then looked at his gray hooded shirt and his blue trousers. "But your clothes are dry."

"It's a long story." He coughed again and slowed his pace.

Bethany realized she was gabbling and felt childish. His cough sounded painful. She reached a hand to his arm. "You sound really ill."

"No, I'm okay."

"Okay," she repeated. "Connor also says that word." When Justin glanced at her hand touching his arm, she saw his face change. Thinking she must seem improper, she removed her hand. "Oh, I'm sorry."

"Don't be." He continued walking beside her. "I haven't seen a woman in a long time—especially one as pretty as you. Is your husband going to be mad at you for helping me?"

"I'm not married. Not that I'm too young—my eighteenth birthday was last week."

He grinned and she liked it. His flawlessly straight teeth gleamed unnaturally. She wanted to stare but forced herself to look away as they stepped off the road and onto the grass. She pointed to the white cottage behind the Colburn house. "Lydia's office is in there."

As they walked across the yard in front of her family's home, Bethany glanced at the stranger named Justin Mercer. He was so different from the men in the Land. Though he was ill, he still seemed strong and even dangerous—in the same way Connor had when he first arrived. Connor always said war raged outside the Land, and she wondered if Justin were the same kind of warrior Connor had been. The thought thrilled her. And Justin's speech was not different from the people in the Land in any nameable way—perhaps in enunciation or simply in the way his mouth moved—but whatever it was, it reminded her of Connor and made her feel an instant connection to Justin.

Bethany knocked on the cottage door, then she turned the knob and crossed the threshold. Justin followed her in, coughing all the while. She glanced back out the open door. "Lydia might be in the house. I'll go look for her." Motioning to the patient cot in the corner of the room, she smiled at him. "You can wait there, if you like."

Justin stepped to the cot but did not sit. He looked around the room, then his eyes settled on Bethany. She could not read his expression but sensed he wanted something. He seemed intent on holding her gaze. Finally, he grinned. "Hurry back, Bethany."

\* \* \*

When Bethany returned to the cottage, Justin was lying on the patient cot. His gray sweater was balled up on the floor, and he wore a white cotton shirt. She held a tray of food with both hands and used her foot to close the door behind her. The noise woke him.

"I'm sorry," she whispered. "I didn't realize you were sleeping. Lydia is still away and Connor isn't home yet. Would you like me to leave you alone so you can rest?"

Justin's grin returned and he raised himself to his elbow. "No, stay. I like talking to you."

The flattery satisfied her. He was charming and mysterious and he liked her. She pressed her lips together then looked at the tray. "I brought food for you."

"You're a saint." Justin sat up and shifted his feet to the floor.

Bethany set the tray on the cot beside him then stepped back and bit her lip, unsure of what to do. She pulled a chair close to the cot and sat. Justin looked at the food, but did not touch it. She watched him for a moment. "Would you like something else?"

He shook his head. "I'm just not that hungry." He gazed at her in a way that made her think he was about to say something, but he only stared.

Feeling awkward, she decided to speak first, so she talked about the only thing they had in common. "Connor and Lydia were married two years ago. They have a son, Andrew, and I think he is quite possibly the most beautiful baby I have ever seen. I'm sure Connor will be happy to see someone from his nation. Were you well acquainted?" When Justin only nodded, she continued. "It was a terrible fright when Connor first arrived. No outsider had ever come here, alive anyway—not since our founders settled here long ago. Connor said no one in the world knew the Land existed and he was adamant that we didn't want the outside world to find us." She stopped speaking as she realized that if Justin made it to the Land, the rest of the warring world could soon follow. "Will others come too?"

"I doubt it." Justin reached for the glass of water on the tray. He drank without pause then held up the empty glass. "This water is perfect."

"Is fresh water still scarce out there?"

"It depends on what you consider fresh." Justin chuckled at his own joke.

Bethany did not understand his meaning, but she liked his voice too much to care. She reached to the jug of water on the tray and refilled his glass. He began to cough again, so she picked up the folded napkin from the tray and handed it to him. "Why are you sick?"

"Everybody's got it." Justin wiped his forehead with the napkin and drew his feet back onto the cot. "I'm going to lie down while we wait for the doctor, but don't leave." He reclined on his side and used his arm for a pillow. His thin shirt had no collar and short sleeves. Bethany stared at the defined muscles in his arms.

"Do you have a boyfriend, Bethany?"

She looked back at his face. "Pardon?"

"You said you weren't married. I just wondered if you have a boyfriend."

"I'm not courting anyone, if that's what you mean."

"Courting?" He looked amused. "Is that what they call it here?"

"Yes." She brushed at the flecks of clay on her skirt, embarrassed of her dirty work clothes. She thought about going into the house to change, but once Lydia arrived she would have to leave the medical office.

"Courting." He whistled one short quiet note as he glanced around the room. "Are you Amish or something like that?"

"No. I don't think I am… that."

He looked back at her and pointed at her head. "Right, you're not wearing the little hat thingy. Where are your people from?"

"Our founders came here from America."

"So this is an American settlement?"

She did not know how to answer him but wanted to appear mature. "I suppose so. What is it like out there?"

"You don't want to know." He rolled onto his back and stared at the ceiling.

Bethany had not been allowed in the medical office when Connor was Lydia's patient, though she had fantasized about it often. She dreamed of a noble warrior falling from the sky and needing her care. As she studied Justin, she wondered if this was what it was like for Lydia. His raucous cough jolted her from her daydream. He covered his mouth with his hand. She wanted to do something to help him. "I'm sorry, I should let you rest while you wait for Lydia—I mean, Doctor Bradshaw."

Justin reached for her hand. "Stay please. It has been so long since I've been with… please stay." He pulled her hand onto his chest and covered it with his.

She knew she should leave so he could rest and for the sake of propriety, but being wanted produced an ineffable pleasure she could not ignore. Bethany's cheeks warmed. "All right, I will stay." She slid to the edge of her seat and let him hold her hand over his heart.

"Thank you." Justin grinned and closed his eyes. "I like your voice. Tell me more about this place. I want to hear all about the Land."

# Chapter Four

Everett strained to hear what Lydia was saying to his mother back in his parents' bedroom. Their muffled words bled through the hallway but dissipated before reaching the parlor. Though his father was dead, Everett felt there was still hope until the doctor officially pronounced it. He stood from the stuffed armchair to pace the parlor floor. Levi and Mandy both looked up at him from where they sat on the divan. Mandy's eyes were red from crying. Levi had his arm behind her and his fingers wrapped securely around her shoulder. Lydia's baby lay sleeping on a knit blanket on the rug beside Mandy's feet.

Everett stepped to the window and pushed his hands through his hair. What was taking so long back there? His father was dead; he had witnessed Samuel's final breath himself. For a moment it had felt like Everett's final breath as well.

His mother's footsteps echoed from the hallway as she walked into the parlor. She held a wet handkerchief to her nose and sniffled. "He's gone. My Samuel is gone." Everett opened his arms, and his mother dropped her head against his chest. "Your father is gone," she sobbed.

Mandy rushed to them and leaned into Everett's side. He took one arm off his weeping mother and wrapped it around his sister. If ever there were a moment where a man's crying would be acceptable, this would be it. He braced for tears, but instead of crying he only felt the urge to inveigh the unfairness of death. Swallowing his bitter protest, he held the weeping women and dredged every ounce of courage he had to be strong for them. He was the man of the house now—the heir to the Foster property—and to lead, he had to be strong.

The baby awoke, but Lydia was still tending to Samuel's body in the back bedroom. Everett watched over the heads of the mourning women as Levi scooped the baby up. Levi carefully supported Andrew's tiny head in his hands. Soon Mandy and Levi would have children too. One generation faded away as another began. Never before had the brevity of life seemed so harsh.

* * *

Justin's chest rose and fell with a steady rhythm, though his breath sounded raspy. Bethany found it awkward to watch a stranger sleep. Lydia was the doctor—the one used to touching people she did not know. Bethany decided Justin was not really a stranger—he was a friend of Connor's and so he was a friend of hers. Besides, he had said he liked her. Surely attraction had the power to void unfamiliarity.

Bethany glanced out the window and saw Connor walking to the main house from the road. She slid her fingers from underneath

Justin's hand, then hurried to the cottage door and stuck her head out. "Connor! You will never believe what's happened!"

Connor coolly turned his face toward her as he continued walking to the house. "Oh, yeah? What's happened now—you find a rocket and a dead Martian or something?" He reached for the knob of the back door.

Bethany glanced back at Justin—he was still asleep on the patient cot. She looked outside at Connor and let out a little squeal. "Come and see for yourself. Oh, you're going to be thrilled! Just come and look!"

Connor smirked at her, making her feel like her enthusiasm was immature. He strode casually to the cottage door. "What are you doing in the medical office anyway?"

Bethany stepped back and motioned with an open palm to the patient cot. "Just look! Another man from your nation!"

"What the—" Connor scowled and pushed the door wide as he rushed past Bethany. The door swung on its hinge and banged into the wall behind it, causing her to jump.

Bethany reached for the door and gently closed it. "Aren't you glad? He said he knows you. His name is Justin Mer—."

"I know his name." Connor hovered over the patient cot and glared at the sleeping man. "Where did he come from?"

Bethany felt guilty, though she had done nothing wrong. "I saw him walking into the village from the shore. He needs a doctor, so I brought him here to wait for Lydia. I found him just like how Lydia found you."

Justin began to stir. He rubbed a hand over his face and opened his eyes. When he saw Connor, he blinked rapidly and sat straight up. "Bradshaw!"

"Lieutenant Mercer. How did you get here?"

Justin stood and embraced Connor, patting him on the back with hearty thuds. "I knew you made it to land! I knew it all along! I saw your chute carry you here. They declared you dead three years ago, but I knew you were here."

Connor stepped back from Justin and returned his fists to his hips. "You saw this land? After the crash?"

"I could only see it during the descent. Once I hit the water, it seemed to vanish." Justin coughed with piercing volume. "Believe me, this place is hard to find," he said as he sat.

Connor crouched in front of the cot. "Who else knows the Land exists?" Justin held up a finger while he coughed again, but Connor continued questioning him. "Mercer, this is important. Who all knows about this place? Who came with you?"

"Only a few sailors, and they're still on the ship"

Connor shot to his feet. "What ship?"

"It's just an icebreaker."

"Could you see the Land from the ship?"

"No." Justin leaned back on his elbows and grinned. "Don't worry about it, Bradshaw. This place is totally off grid—it's practically invisible. It doesn't show up on satellite, radar, nothing. No one believed me when I reported seeing land after the crash. They searched awhile then gave up. The navy thought I was crazy—sent me to McMurdo Station in Antarctica to monitor satellite feeds." He heaved a sigh. "You wouldn't believe what I went through to get back here."

Bethany watched the reunion and the flurry of questions between the men. She smiled and took a step closer, hoping to be drawn into the exciting conversation. "How did you get here, Justin?" she asked. Both of the men glanced at Bethany, but they immediately returned their attention to each other without answering her.

Connor and Justin spoke of technical things Bethany did not understand. Justin sat forward as if he was going to tell Connor a secret. He rested his forearms on his thighs and lowered his voice. "Shortly after I was transferred to McMurdo Station, all satellite communications went down. But the crazy thing is: I ended up getting out here with the help of the same guy who was contracted to sabotage the Unified States communications. Turns out, Washington's number one enemy is actually a pretty cool guy. Anyway, while I was at McMurdo, I saw how the South Atlantic Anomaly played a part in the atmospheric phenomenon I was detecting near the crash coordinates but then the comm links went down. When I finally made it off Antarctica, I met Volt in the Falklands and he had this idea that we—"

"Volt?" Connor interrupted.

"Yeah, Volt. You've heard of him." Justin stopped to cough. "He put a skeleton crew together and we took the icebreaker. We must've crossed the crash coordinates a dozen times before our engines lost power. And we never saw any land. I'd almost given up, but when the fever set in yesterday, I knew I had to get off that ship." Justin chuckled. "I passed out in the dinghy, floated west, and woke up here this morning. Can you believe it? Of all the luck!"

"Fever?" Connor's voice dropped an octave and rose in decibels. "What fever?"

"T.B.—everybody has it. It's some mutated strain."

"Tuberculosis? Are you kidding me?" Connor raked his fingers through his hair. "Mercer, you can't spread disease to these people. There are no contagious diseases here. The people that settled this place quarantined themselves before they left America in eighteen-sixty. They haven't been sick in seven generations. Their immune systems couldn't handle the sniffles. I was immunized against tuberculosis when I was in Arizona, but you're going to kill everyone else."

Justin scooted back on the cot and rubbed his palms on his blue pants. "Look, I'm sorry. How was I supposed to know I'd actually make it here? Besides, I'm going to be dead soon. I've watched half our crew die of this in the past few months and some of them died within days of the fever."

Connor paced the floor. A vein bulged in his neck. "I've got a family here, Mercer. My wife and I just had a son."

"I'm sorry." Justin coughed and put a hand over his chest. "In the Falklands they said this was a virulent strain, so I'll probably be dead by morning and you won't have to worry about it. Just hide me somewhere and let me die in peace. No one will catch it."

Connor turned to Bethany. "How long have you been in here with him?" His expression was a terrifying mix of anger and grief. "Answer me!"

She took a step back. "I, I don't know… an hour, maybe two."

Justin took his hand off his chest. "Oh, man, I'm sorry."

Both men looked at her with pity as if she were a little girl who just fell in the mud. Her desire to be seen as a sophisticated adult vanished, and she only wanted to run to the house and cry. She swallowed the lump in her throat. "What? What did I do wrong?"

Connor's heels thumped the floor as he stepped close to her. She covered her face with her hands. He wrapped his fingers around her wrists and gently pulled her hands down. When she looked into his eyes, he inclined his head. "Did you touch him?"

Bethany sniffed. "Only a little." She dragged a knuckle under her eye to wipe her tears. "Can't Lydia just give him tea from the gray leaf tree? That will help him, right?"

"It's not him I'm worried about." Connor's nostrils flared as he stepped back. He turned his face toward the house. "Lydia can't come inside this cottage. And Bethany, you can't leave."

"What do you mean?"

"You've been exposed to a deadly bacteria. You're probably already infected. If you leave this cottage, you will spread it to others."

"I don't understand. Something deadly is in me?" Her heart began to pound inside her chest. "What does that mean? Connor, what is going on?"

"Lydia is coming. Just go upstairs."

"Connor—"

"Go!"

Bethany's breath caught between sobs as she stomped up the stairs to Lydia's old bedroom. When she heard Connor open the cottage door and speak to Lydia, she stopped and sat on the steps to listen. She wrapped her arms around her knees and tried to suppress her crying so she could hear what Connor was saying.

The afternoon sun flooded through the crack in the door as Connor spoke to Lydia outside. Bethany could see a sliver of Lydia's figure. She was holding Andrew in one arm and pressed the other palm against her abdomen. Bethany heard the tension in Connor's voice as he explained the situation. Lydia murmured a worried response. Andrew started to cry and Bethany wondered if the baby felt his parent's angst. She wanted to run down the stairs and comfort Andrew and tell him everything would be fine, but Connor said she had something deadly in her—whatever that meant—and she did not want to expose the baby.

Connor opened the door a little wider but postured himself at the threshold. Bethany looked past him and saw Lydia's face. When Lydia's eyes met hers, she started to cry.

"Bethany?" Connor raised his voice. "Did you hear me?"

Bethany shook her head, unable to utter a word through her sobs.

"I'm going to get the dinghy off the beach so no one touches it. Lydia is going to make gray leaf tea for Mercer, then she's going to the library to see what she can find out about treating consumption from the founders' journals. Do not come down those stairs, you understand me?"

Bethany nodded. Connor turned to the patient cot and pointed sharply in Justin's direction. "My wife is making gray leaf tea for you. It's the only medicine here. When it's ready, she will knock on the door and leave it on the doorstep. Drink it all and get back to that cot to lie down before it kicks in. The gray leaf is powerful and like nothing you've ever had. Whatever you do, Lieutenant Mercer, don't leave this cottage. Got it?"

Bethany could not see Justin from where she sat on the top step, but she heard him chuckle. "Yeah, is that an order Lieutenant Bradshaw?"

Connor ignored Justin's remark and looked up at Bethany. His voice softened. "Beth, Lydia needs to tell you something before you go in the room."

Lydia drew her lips into her mouth and nodded. She shifted Andrew in her arms and patted his back to calm him. Then she tilted her head up toward Bethany. "Samuel died."

Bethany's thoughts turned from fear for herself to grief over Samuel. Struck by the loss of a man who was like a second father to her and the depth of pain she knew was suffocating Everett and Mandy and Roseanna, she rushed into Lydia's old bedroom and threw herself on the bed, weeping.

* * *

Bethany stared out the upstairs window of the medical cottage. Her unfocused vision blurred the image of the gray leaf trees' black silhouettes against the western sky's fading lavender light. Her arms—twined through the decorative iron headboard on Lydia's old bed—began to tingle from being in one position for so long. Her tears had dried, but she doubted she would ever smile again. When Connor tapped on the frame of the open bedroom door, Bethany lifted her cheek from the cool metal of the headboard and peeled her gaze away from the lonely view of the western sky.

"Hungry?" he asked, holding a covered dinner plate.

Bethany shook her head, then she turned her face back to the window. Connor set the plate on the bedside table and the mattress lowered as he sat beside her. "Look, Beth, I'm sorry you can't go to the funeral tomorrow. I know how much Samuel meant to you, but it's too dangerous for the village. You don't want to get people sick."

"What did Lydia find out from the medical journals?" Her dry throat burned when she spoke.

"You and Mercer have to stay quarantined for a few days—"

"A few days?" She snapped her face toward Connor. "Why so long?"

"We don't have the technology here to test you for infection. All we can do is watch for symptoms. We won't know if the gray leaf will kill this type of bacteria until we see how Mercer's body responds to the tea."

"Will you get sick?"

"No, I was vaccinated against this disease as a child. There was an outbreak where I lived, and the doctors gave me medicine that helped my body build immunity to the disease. But you and your family and everyone else in the Land could get just as sick as Mercer. That's why we have to be careful."

Bethany did not understand. "I just want it to go away. Is Justin feeling better?"

"He's still asleep. I can't tell yet if the gray leaf is helping. Lydia has been relaying medical orders to me through the door, but I'm not as good at this as she is. I guess we'll know more when he wakes up." Connor put his palm on Bethany's back. His hand was wide and warm. "Are you going to be okay up here by yourself?"

Bethany did not respond but only studied Connor. His brow was furrowed, his eyes held concern, and his voice sounded low and worn. He was worried about her, but she was not worried about herself anymore. She only wanted to be there for Everett when his father was buried, but instead an invisible threat imprisoned her in the unused bedroom of the medical cottage. She stared out the window. The night's first star appeared in the sky; the tears in her eyes turned its prick of light into a ribbon.

Connor gave her back a soft pat, then he stood. He walked away from the bed in the darkening room. His footsteps stopped at the door. "Lydia is getting your clothes and the sketchbooks you asked for. I'll go out and light the log beneath the rain tank so you have warm water to bathe. I know you're upset, but you really should eat."

She glanced at Connor. Her lingering childish nature told her to resent the man who was forcing her to remain locked away, but she sensed his compassion for her and ignored her desire to pout. "Thank you, Connor."

He nodded once and left the room. She heard him descend the stairs and leave the cottage. A few minutes later, he returned with a stack of clothes, her favorite pillow, and a satchel. Her sketchbook and pencil box were tucked under his elbow. "Hey, it's kind of like you get to have your own place for a few days," he joked.

Bethany was not in the mood to laugh. Connor deposited her belongings onto the bed and stepped back. He glanced at the untouched plate of food on the bedside table but did not say anything about it. He walked to the doorway of the washroom opposite the bed and leaned his head in. "The water should be warm soon, if you want to take a bath. I think Lydia packed everything you'll need in that bag. I'm going downstairs, but I'll check on you before bed. Okay?"

Bethany nodded and Connor pulled the bedroom door closed as he left. She scooped the clothes into her arms, carried them to the narrow dresser that stood against the wall, and shoved them into an empty drawer. Then she opened the satchel and dumped its contents onto the mattress. Her pocket-sized Bible fell onto the stack that poured from the bag. Then out dropped a thick piece of folded gray leaf paper. Bethany unfolded the paper and found the silver charm bracelet Levi had given her years before. In her brother's hurried script, the note read: Dear Beth, I am sorry I was not there to protect you. Levi.

Bethany looped the bracelet around her wrist and fastened its clasp. She watched the silver links catch the lantern light as she gathered the things she needed and carried the lantern into the washroom.

* * *

The muscles in Everett's back ached from a long evening of farm chores. He propped his pitchfork against the barn door, then he led his father's favorite horse into a freshly cleaned stall. He stroked a hand across the horse's shoulder. It was not his father's horse anymore. Samuel was dead and would be buried in the morning. The mare was Everett's now. He loved the horse but loathed the thought of owning it because that meant he had lost his father. Though he always knew he would one day inherit the family farm, he never imagined it would happen when he was only twenty.

Everett left the mare and carried his lantern into the next stall to check on its colt. Though the five-month-old colt had been weaned, it tried to push past him to get to the mare. As he held the colt back and closed the stall gate, someone entered the barn.

"Everett?"

"In here," he called as he leaned out the stall and saw Levi walking into the darkened barn. "Did you and John get everything… done?"

"Yes. The gravesite is ready." Levi skirted the stall gate and held a hand out to the colt.

"I wanted to help, but you and John were right: my mother needed me here." Everett lifted the lantern and hung it on a hook in the middle of the barn stall. He glanced at Levi and saw the dirt stains on his clothes from digging the grave. "Has Mandy gone home, or is she still in the house with my mother?"

"She is still here." Levi crossed his arms. "Listen, Everett... something has happened."

Everett took a currycomb from a shelf on the wall and began to brush the colt. "Besides my father's death?"

"Yes."

"What is it?"

Levi drew a deep breath. "The man who was in Connor's aircraft with him is here in Good Springs. Apparently, the Land is undetectable to the outside world, but this man saw it after they were ejected from the aircraft. No one believed him about seeing land, but he spent the past three years trying to get back here and he finally made it."

Everett stopped brushing the colt. "Did he come here alone?"

"There are four men still on his ship, but they can't see the Land. He came to the shore alone."

Everett nodded. "What's his name?"

"Mercer. Justin Mercer."

"It sounds like this Mercer has perseverance. Is Connor happy about it?"

"No."

"Why not?"

Levi shoved his hands into his pockets. "Mercer is sick."

"Oh. That's too bad."

"The disease Mercer has is contagious. He says a lot of people in the outside world are sick right now. But that's not the worst of it."

Everett pulled a clump of hair out of the horse brush then looked at Levi. "Is it deadly?"

"Yes, and Bethany might be infected."

"What?" The news hit Everett in the gut like a fast kick. Anger deluged his system and swelled his grief-stricken heart. He spun on his heel and threw the wood-handled brush against the barn wall. The forceful clap sent the colt scurrying to the back of the stall.

Levi did not flinch. "Beth was the first person to see Mercer. He has a bad cough, and she spent the afternoon with him in the medical office," he explained. "Connor said they had been in there together for a couple of hours by the time he got there. Connor can't catch the disease because he had some medicine that made him immune to it when he was a child, but Bethany probably breathed it in while she was with Mercer. No one else has been exposed."

Everett's father was dead and the woman he loved was possibly infected with a deadly disease. Overwhelmed, he bent at the waist and leaned his hands on his knees. "Where is she now?"

"Upstairs of the medical cottage."

"I have to go to her."

"You can't."

"Why not?"

"Lydia has them quarantined. Bethany and Mercer have to stay inside the cottage and only Connor can go in. Otherwise, the whole village could become infected."

Everett's eyes stung. He did not bother fighting back his angry tears. "For how long?" Levi did not answer. Everett raised his body and doubled his volume. "For how long?"

Levi spoke through barely parted lips. "Until it's over for them."

# Chapter Five

Bethany gripped the edge of the tub as she lowered herself into the warm water. Her silver charm bracelet clinked when it touched the porcelain of the bathtub. Resting her head against the papered wall behind the tub, she glanced around the washroom and remembered how envious she had been when her father and Levi built the pretty cottage for Lydia. With the medical office downstairs and Lydia's private room upstairs, the purpose of the cottage was for Lydia to be available when anyone in the village needed care, but Bethany had wished they would build a cottage for her too. And when Connor arrived and fell in love with Lydia, Bethany thought life unjust. She remembered how—at only fifteen—she thought Connor was the most perfect man she had ever encountered. While Lydia took her time considering the possibility of sharing her life with Connor, Bethany had burned with envy, desperate to be loved by such a brave and courteous man. Now Lydia was happily married to Connor, and Bethany had grown out of her jealousy. Instead of dreaming of Connor, she now watched the love between him and Lydia and dreamed of finding a love like theirs someday.

As Bethany began to fantasize about being loved, she thought of Justin. The charming and mysterious outsider was downstairs, asleep and ill. He had said he liked the sound of her voice. Though she had only just met him, she liked him too. She hummed as she recalled the feeling of his chest beneath her hand. A wave of dizziness swayed her vision. She blinked and the strong and strange sensation went away. Maybe such a powerful physical reaction to a thought about a person had some deep and instructive meaning. Before she could delve into the notion, the dizziness returned. It was not a swoon of emotion, but a warning from her body. Sitting up, she reached for a rag to dab her face. As the soft cloth absorbed drips from her forehead, more ran down. She had not yet wet her hair and the tub water was not hot enough to produce steam. Bethany glanced to the ceiling, wondering why her head was so wet. As she lifted her chin, the dizziness returned with full force. Her ears began to ring and her heart pounded with hard, irregular thumps.

Bethany pulled the plug and clung to the side of the tub as the water swirled down the drain. She began to shiver even though she was not cold. Clenching her eyes shut, she reached her fingers to the floor outside the tub and found her towel. Her teeth began to chatter as she clambered out. She knelt on the floor and willed her shaky fingers to open her nightgown and pull it over her head.

Overcome with dizziness, she curled her legs beneath her body and buried her spinning head in the damp towel. Maybe she had caught the deadly illness. Panic set in. Her throat tightened and her breath came in painful, shallow spurts. She lifted herself to her knees and crawled across the painted wood floor to the washroom door. Her vision blurred as she looked up at the glass knob on the door, so she closed her eyes and turned it.

The dark bedroom felt eerily empty. Her head began to throb as she glanced back into the bathroom where the lantern's warm light glowed from the shelf above the sink. The lantern was out of reach and she did not trust her shaking legs enough to stand. As she crawled into the darkened bedroom, streams of the lantern's orange light trailed through her blurred vision. She squeezed her eyes shut and dropped her aching head to the floor. Through the piercing that rang in her ears, she thought she heard Connor downstairs. She coiled her fist and pounded it against the floorboards, desperate for help. Every knock she produced sent jarring pain through her body.

The door opened. Connor's voice came from above her. She could not see him. He was close, but the sound of his voice was faint like an echo in the distance. "Beth? Are you all right? What happened?"

As she lifted her head from the floor, sweat dripped into her eyes. Connor's hands pressed on her shoulders and she tried to answer, but her mouth would not move. Her eyes felt detached from her body and refused to focus on anything.

"Bethany? Oh no, you caught it! Can you hear me?" He scooped her from the floor. "I've got you. You're going to be okay. Can you hear me?" He kept talking and she wanted to hear his words just to know he was there, but every sound felt like a dagger jabbing into her already aching brain.

Connor laid her on the bed and put his hand on her forehead. "You're burning up. It's not supposed to happen this fast. I've got to tell Lydia. She'll know what to do. I'll be right back. Bethany? I'll be right back, okay?"

She tried to respond, but her breath stung her constricted throat. Connor left the room. She did not want to be alone. Her lungs felt like they were filled with fire. She rubbed her quivering fingers across the bedsheet and they dampened with the moisture that leaked from her sweating body. Then a hand was beneath her head, lifting her onto the pillow. She heard a voice, deep and muffled, and tried to focus on it.

"Bethany, you have to drink this."

The pungent aroma of steeped gray leaf wafted across her face. Her stomach churned. "No."

"Drink it, Bethany. Mercer is awake and he feels better. We think the gray leaf will heal this disease, but you have to drink the tea."

She could hear Connor and wanted healing, but her tongue felt swollen inside her dry mouth. She could not will her mouth to move but was able to open her eyes. Lantern light glowed from the bedside table. It illuminated Connor's worried face and the porcelain cup he held close to her lips. Then everything went black.

"You have to drink this." He pressed the cup to her lips. "Just swallow."

She let the cup part her lips and the hot tea poured over her tongue. The tea tasted bitter, but not as unpleasant as she had always imagined it would be. She swallowed and the heat of the tea passed through her throat and into her stomach. After another sip she stopped and caught her breath. "I want my father."

"He can't come in here. He's really worried about you, Beth, but he can't come in here or he will catch it too. Please, drink all of this."

She looked at Connor's begging eyes. If she did not finish the tea, she had no hope of fighting off the disease. Her chin quivered. "I don't want to die."

"I don't want you to die either. Drink the tea."

Bethany forced herself to take another sip and when she did, heat rose again inside her body, but not from the temperature of the tea or from the crippling fever. This heat was different, and it lured her to swallow again and again until the cup was empty. The sensation spread through her, calming her shaking muscles and easing her staggered breath.

As Connor drew the empty cup away, Bethany's vision cleared except for little flecks of white light that twinkled in the periphery. She took a slow, deep breath and when she exhaled, the pain that burned her lungs dissipated. Her ears stopped ringing and the headache dissolved. As the gray leaf tree's healing properties flowed through her body, fatigue overtook her. Her head dropped to the soft pillow.

Connor sat on the edge of the bed and hovered over her, studying her. "Bethany?"

"Yes." She breathed the word through unmoving lips.

"You stopped shaking." He wiped a rag across her forehead. "Do you feel better?"

"I want to live."

He gave a short chuckle that sounded like it was part sob. "Then fight this disease. I think the gray leaf will help, but you have to fight."

She liked the warmth brought by the gray leaf medicine. It reminded her of her mother. She missed her mother. If she did die she would get to see her mother again. She liked the thought. It would be all white light and peace and angels singing. But it was too soon. She wanted to go back to the pottery and make all of the things she had dreamed of making. She wanted to sit at the kitchen table in her father's house and eat and laugh with her family. She wanted to see her friends marry and have children. She wanted to see Everett. Though she tried to lift her head, it would not budge. She looked at Connor. "I want to be loved."

He drew his head back a degree. "You are loved. Your family loves you so much… and your friends… this whole village. You father is gathering the elders right now. Half the village will be awake praying for you all night. You are loved."

Knowing the village was praying for her gave her hope, but that was not the kind of love she meant. Her eyelids began to close against her will. "No, I mean by a man. I want to be loved by a man—the way you love Lydia. That's all I've ever wanted."

Bethany's breathing settled into a smooth, shallow rhythm and as she slipped into sleep, she heard Connor's kind voice. "You will be loved like that one day, Beth. You will."

* * *

The glow of morning light seeped through Bethany's eyelids. She drew her pillow over her head and hoped to return to a particularly pleasant dream, then she remembered where she was. She peeked one eye open to confirm she was in the upstairs room of Lydia's medical cottage. The reality of that horrid illness flooded her mind, and she drew the quilt to her chin. The gray leaf tea seemed to have removed all trace of the symptoms—save for exhaustion.

The bedroom door creaked, causing Bethany to open both eyes. Connor held a coffee cup in one hand and closed the door with the other. He gave her a quick glance. "Hey, you're awake."

Bethany could smell the coffee from across the room. She took a deep breath. "That smells heavenly."

"Want some?"

"I don't drink coffee. I like the smell but not the taste."

"I know. I just thought maybe your tastes changed after getting a second lease on life." Connor grinned as he walked to a chair near the bed. "How do you feel?"

"Better. Tired but better." Bethany rolled onto her side and watched Connor as he sat. She didn't remember a chair being in the room. "Have you been up here all night?"

"Of course."

"Thank you."

He took a sip from the mug and looked at her through the steam. "You're welcome."

"How is my father?"

"He's grateful that you survived."

"Has Justin fully recovered?"

"He's better. Lydia thinks his lungs will need another day to heal, but it looks like the gray leaf can beat this. She said this form of tuberculosis is different from what the founders wrote about seeing in America. It took you down fast. Mercer said that's how it affected a lot of people in the outside world. They don't have the medicine to keep up with it."

"I would have died if you hadn't acted so quickly, wouldn't I?"

Connor shrugged. "Probably."

Bethany sat up and leaned against the cool iron headboard. "Since I'm better now, can I go into the house?"

"No, we still have to keep you quarantined. Lydia made a sanitizer out of gray leaf oil and we're using it on everything, but there is no way to know if the bacteria are dead. We just have to wait it out."

Bethany hated being forced to stay indoors. Wanting to go to the pottery and feel the clay in her hands, she glanced at her pigment stained nails. "How long will I have to stay in here?"

Connor tipped his cup high, draining the last drop. He set it on the side table. His brow contracted as he folded his hands in his lap. "Ten days." When Bethany groaned, he leaned forward and braced his elbows on his knees. "You don't want to risk getting anyone else as sick as you were last night. This would kill Andrew. I know you don't want to be stuck in here for ten days, but we think it's the only way to make sure no one else gets sick."

Bethany thought of her father and siblings and little Andrew. She would do whatever it took to protect them from the illness. She nodded. "That's fine. Whatever you and Lydia say is right, I'm sure."

Connor leaned back in the chair. "That's a very mature attitude." He brushed his palms together then reached for his empty cup and stood. "I'll go tell everyone you're awake. Levi and Mandy were here before the sun came up.

Mandy made breakfast; I'll bring some back for you."

As Connor walked to the door, Bethany remembered Samuel's death and her grief returned. "Is the burial this morning?"

Connor stopped and looked back at her. He put his hand against the doorframe. "It's at noon. I'm sorry, Beth, but you can't go." When she wrapped the quilt around her hands, Connor inclined his head. "Do you need me to stay here with you?"

Bethany thought about the expectation in the village—every person was to show respect by attending a funeral service. She could think of no one outside her family that she respected more than Samuel Foster. She could not go, but she would not keep anyone else away. Bethany shook her head. "You must go. I'll be fine, really. Just please tell Everett I'm sorry."

* * *

Everett stared at the dirt being shoveled over his father's casket. Tears slid down his face as he watched two men rhythmically cast more soil into the grave. The stems of the mourners' flowers quickly disappeared beneath the dirt. The fragmented shadow of a nearby gray leaf tree dispelled the early afternoon sun as the mourners silently left the graveside. John Colburn whispered condolences to Samuel Foster's relatives as they filed away.

Everett peeled his unfocused gaze from the grave and glanced at Connor. Before their eyes could meet, he looked back at the dirt. Connor put a hand on his shoulder. Neither man spoke. They did not need to. After a moment, Connor gave Everett's shoulder a squeeze then turned and walked away.

Everett stood somberly between his mother and sister. Roseanna's hands shook as she dabbed her eyes with a scallop-edged handkerchief. Mandy's unrestrained cries pierced the air. Levi wrapped his arm around her waist and ushered her away from the grave. Roseanna turned and followed them through the shadowy grass, weeping.

Everett looked at the grave as the men patted the dirt with the backs of their spades. In time the dirt would settle, but for now his father's coffin swelled the earth unnaturally. Everett heard footsteps in the grass and glanced back as John came to stand beside him. The dark skin beneath the overseer's eyes attested to the long night he had endured because of Bethany's sickness.

John thanked the men as they walked away with their shovels, and then he looked at Everett. "What can I do to help you through this, son?"

Everett felt childish for having cried. He cleared his throat. "I don't need help."

"You will. You now own the largest property in Good Springs. Your herd nearly doubled this year. And your father was a village elder. That is quite an inheritance for a young man."

"I have hired two men and I will hire another soon. And I'm prepared for the training to be an elder." Everett did not want to talk about the weight of his new responsibilities as he looked at his father's fresh grave. "Connor told me Bethany got sick last night and she's better now, but I know whatever happened was more serious than Connor described." He turned to John. "Is she still in danger?"

John cleared his throat. "She is weak but appears to have overcome the worst of it. The gray leaf tea worked against the illness, but Lydia believes it is imperative that they remain quarantined. There must be no symptoms for ten days before she will release them."

"And then what?" Everett felt a surge of anger. "What will we do with this Mercer?"

John's eyes narrowed. "Justin Mercer was Connor's colleague. He searched for three years to find this Land. I do not believe he is wrong in coming here."

"He made Bethany sick. She could have died, John." Everett glanced at Samuel's grave and lowered his voice. "I don't like the thought of them being in the cottage together for ten days."

"Nor do I. We have to trust Connor to handle this. He is the only person immune to this disease and he saved Bethany's life last night. He will watch out for her." John put his hand to Everett's shoulder. "I know you love her, son."

John's paternal demeanor reminded Everett of his father. He looked away. "Yes, I do."

"I do too and staying out of that cottage last night took every ounce of self-restraint I had. I know she is eighteen, but she is still my little girl. If I can trust Connor to protect her, so can you."

* * *

Though it was only noon on the first day of the quarantine, Bethany already felt restless being confined to the upstairs bedroom of the cottage. In cautious movements, she slid her weak legs over the edge of the bed, then kept her hands on the mattress as she stood. She waited for the lightness in her head to pass before she straightened her nightgown and stepped to the window. The sun-filled yard below beckoned her, and the sash window creaked as she raised it. She stuck her head out and inhaled the salty ocean air. A cool breeze moved the edges of the curtains as it swirled into her prison.

She turned away from the window and scanned the room for her sketchbook. The mountain of personal belongings she had dumped on the bed the day before was now a neat stack atop the dresser. Bethany pulled her sketchbook and pencil box from beneath the carefully arranged items and wondered if Lydia's organizational skills had rubbed off on Connor or if his care for a person extended to her possessions. She carried her sketchbook and pencils to the bed. While she flipped through her old drawings, she heard Justin call to her from downstairs.

"Bethany?"

She turned her head toward the closed door. "Yes?" When he did not respond, she assumed her tired voice was too weak to carry through the cottage. She rose and inched to the door then cracked it open. "Justin?"

"Are you feeling better?" His voice came from the medical office below, but she could not see him.

She opened the door a bit wider. "Yes. Are you?"

"Yeah. That gray leaf tea is something else, isn't it?"

"What do you mean?"

"It felt amazing. It knocked me out and I woke up feeling great."

"Oh, yes. It helped me, too." The walk to the door had drained her energy. She leaned against the wall. "But I'm still weak."

She heard Justin moving around downstairs. His voice sounded closer. "I'm really sorry about that, by the way."

"About what?"

"Getting you sick."

"It wasn't your fault. You didn't know you could infect other people." Justin was silent for a moment and Bethany thought he was done talking. She stepped away from the door and shuffled back to the bed. As she picked up her sketchbook, she heard him again.

"Bethany?"

"Yes?" She moved to the door, hugging her sketchbook to her chest.

"I did know. I mean, I didn't want to make anyone sick, but I knew how contagious it was. It was just that once I met you, I wanted you to stay with me. I thought I was going to die and I didn't want to die alone. Do you hate me now?"

The thought of dying alone struck her and she felt sorry for him. She lowered herself to the floor and rested her back against the wall by the door. "Of course not."

"So you forgive me?"

She turned her face to the chink in the door. "Yes."

"Come down here and talk to me."

"Connor told me to stay up here." She opened her sketchbook and laid it in her lap. As she selected a graphite pencil and stared at the blank page awaiting inspiration, she heard movement on the stairs. She peeked through the crack in the door and saw Justin sit on the second step from the bottom. He leaned his head against the wall and looked up at the door. She pulled her face out of view and believed she went unseen.

"How long do funerals last around here?" he asked.

Bethany heard his words but found his question strange. She smoothed the paper on her sketchbook. "There will be a memorial service in the chapel and then my father will speak at the gravesite before the burial. So a couple of hours, I suppose. Why?"

"Why will your dad speak? Were they close?"

"They were, but my father always speaks at funerals; he is the overseer of Good Springs."

"Is that like a mayor of the town?"

"I guess. He leads the elder meetings and preaches sermons and officiates weddings."

"You make Good Springs sound more like a church than a town."

"I guess it's both." Bethany swirled her pencil across the page in more of a mindless doodle than an intentional design.

"Were you close to the guy who died?"

Her pencil stopped and she looked at the open window. "Yes. The Fosters are like family to me. Samuel was like another father or an uncle, I suppose. I feel terrible that I could not go and pay my respects today. Or be there for Mandy and Everett."

"Who?"

"Mandy and Everett—Samuel's daughter and son. Mandy is married to my brother, Levi, and Everett is my... I don't know how to describe him... my best friend, I guess. Only..."

"Only what?"

"There's more to it than that."

Justin chuckled. "Do you have a thing for him?"

"No… I was intrigued with him when we were in school, if that's what you mean. But he's older than me, and I don't think he feels that way about me." Bethany looked back at the page and started doodling again. "Then last year, I was attacked and it was Everett who saved me."

"Ah, so now he's your hero."

Bethany smiled and drew a looping vine along the edge of the page. "Yes, in a way. But the whole ordeal made him very serious."

"About you?"

"No, it just changed him somehow. It made him more protective of me. He's still my dearest friend, but I think he sees me differently now… like a little sister to watch over. And once Samuel became ill, Everett had to work a lot more so I don't see him very often. When he isn't working he is usually with Levi or Connor. I wanted to be with him today. Just knowing he is hurting and I can't go to him makes me sad."

She stopped sketching and turned to a blank page. "Tell me about your airplane—the one you and Connor were flying when you first saw the Land."

Justin was quiet for a moment. "I didn't see the Land from the aircraft. I saw it during the parachute descent." He cleared his throat and spoke in a barely audible voice. "What do you want to know about it?"

The change in his tone made Bethany turn her head toward the door. Certain she heard pain in his voice, she wished she could see his face. She considered opening the door, but she glanced at her sweat-stained nightgown and decided she did not want him to see her. She looked back at the page. "Describe it to me. I want to try to draw it."

"Describe it? You mean you've never seen an airplane?" Justin asked, but she did not answer, keeping the secret of the old plane that was buried below the bluffs. "Okay, um, imagine a bird—maybe a sea gull—but with straight wings and smooth contours. The aircraft in our squadron are electronic warfare aircraft—they are sleek and aerodynamic machines—so think long, lean lines. And they're big. Do your people measure in feet or meters?"

"Feet."

"The type of aircraft we were flying that day is sixty feet long and sixteen feet high. Its nose is thin and comes to a point. The crew sits in tandem in the cockpit, which is about where the head is on a bird. The aviator's seat is in the forward cockpit and the weapon systems officer sits in the rear. A clear canopy seals them inside. The aircraft's wings begin behind the middle of the craft, and it also has a pair of outwardly slanted vertical tail fins. It's powered by twin turbofan engines that exhaust to the back of the aircraft through two rings. And imagine several tube-shaped pods under the wings. They hold the aircraft's wing tanks, tactical jamming—sorry, I'm getting too technical—"

"No, keep going." Bethany's pencil made quick swipes as she poured the image onto the page. "I like to hear about it. Do the airplane's wings flap like a bird?"

Justin chuckled. "No, the wings are fixed. Jet engines propel the aircraft."

Bethany sketched the wings as she imagined them and used the tip of her middle finger to shade the graphite. "How fast can it fly?"

"Almost twelve hundred miles per hour."

"I can't imagine that. Do you miss flying?"

Justin did not respond. The only sound in the cottage was the scratching of Bethany's pencil across the page. She finished the sketch and tore the page from the book, then she peeked at him through the crack in the door. He was still sitting on the second step from the bottom, only he had turned the other way.

Bethany slid the drawing under the door. She heard the paper graze the steps and then crackle when Justin picked it up.

"Nice sketch. It's actually pretty close." He sounded surprised. "You're a good artist."

Bethany grinned, liking his approval. She leaned her head against the doorframe. "I'm a potter."

"That explains the dirt."

"What dirt?"

"You were a mess when I met you yesterday. At first I thought you were a peasant girl."

Her face felt warm like she was blushing. She was glad he could not see her. "Oh, sorry. I had just left the pottery yard."

"Don't apologize. You looked beautiful."

Her mouth dropped open. She sat still—her back leaning against the wall, her face turned to the crack in the door, her sketchbook resting on her lap—and absorbed his compliment. As she considered how to respond, she heard the cottage door open and then Connor spoke to Justin. Connor said Samuel's funeral was over and asked how Justin was feeling. She heard

Connor say he was going into the house and would be right back. Then the cottage door closed.

"Hey, are you still by the door?" Justin's voice came from the bottom of the stairs. She heard the sound of paper crinkling.

"Yes."

"Open the door."

"No, I look terrible."

"Just open it a little more and stay back."

Bethany smiled and pushed the door open a few inches with her fingers. She waited, curious as to what Justin planned to do. Something flew into the room. It caused her to flinch, but then she saw it was her sketch paper folded into the shape of an airplane. The paper airplane circled past the dresser and lowered to the floor before sliding nose first into the baseboard near her. She giggled and reached for it then heard Connor enter the cottage. Bethany closed the bedroom door and smiled while holding the fascinating paper airplane.

# Chapter Six

Everett propped his weary feet on the empty kitchen chair across from him. Roseanna was leaning over the sink where she had been scouring the same pan for several minutes. Unable to bear the scratching noises any longer, Everett stood from the table and carried his empty plate to the sink. "Thanks for dinner, Mother. It was great."

Roseanna nodded without making eye contact, then continued scrubbing the pan over the sudsy water. Everett walked to the back door and looked out the window into the darkened yard. His thoughts had remained fixed on Bethany since he first heard about Mercer and the illness. Though Everett was filled with grief for his father and busy with the work of the farm, he had spent the past five days tormented by the image of Bethany locked away with a man he had never met. He glanced at his mother. "I'm going to the Colburn house, that is, if you'll be all right alone."

Roseanna looked up at him. "I'll be fine, son. You should go. I know you're worried about sweet Bethany. I am too."

"Do you want to come with me?"

"No, no." She grinned slightly then returned her attention to the sparkling pan. "I need time alone."

"You have been alone all day. Are you sure you don't want to go?"

"Quite sure." Roseanna glanced at him then back at the dishes. She forced a smile as she scrubbed. "It's good for me to be alone now. I'm settling into my grief. That is something a widow has to get used to. Don't worry about me. You have enough to think about. Give the Colburns my best. I'll leave the lamp on the table for you."

Everett grabbed his coat from the rack by the back door and shrugged into its woolen sleeves as he stepped outside. Shep trudged down the porch steps and hobbled beside Everett through the yard. The dog stopped at the edge of the road as Everett left his property and walked to the village. The cool air and the mile walk did little to calm his anxious mind.

The oval-shaped moon lit the Colburn property as Everett stepped off the road and walked toward the house. He did not need the light; he could have walked straight to the familiar back door in complete darkness if he had to. He glanced at the cottage. Gauzy curtains obscured his view into the medical office, but the firelight lit the windows. The man called Mercer was in there with Bethany—his Bethany.

Everett knocked lightly on the Colburns' back door then turned the knob. John was sitting at the head of the kitchen table with his Bible open in his palm. He glanced up at Everett. "Come in, son."

Everett stepped into the warm kitchen. The house was quiet except for the faint scuff of footsteps upstairs. He looked at the Bible in the overseer's hand. "I'm sorry to interrupt your study."

"Not at all." John slid the Bible onto the table. "Hang up your coat and have a seat. Can I get you anything?"

Everett shook his head as he hung his coat on one of several brass hooks screwed into the wall behind the door. He rubbed his cold hands together as he walked to the table. "How is Bethany?"

"She is like a caged bird—bored and restless." John smiled. "But she has fully recovered from the illness, so we are thankful no matter her temperament."

"Have you been able to talk to her?"

John crossed his legs, ankle over knee. "Yes, she has become fond of yelling from the upstairs window."

"How about this Mercer fellow? Have you met him?"

"Connor introduced us through the door."

Everett lowered himself into the chair nearest John. "What is he like?"

"I would not want to judge a man when we have only been introduced through a door."

Everett appreciated John's fairness, but knew the overseer had a way of seeing through pretenses. He leaned forward. "My father always said that you are good at sizing up a man's character the moment you meet him. When Connor first arrived, my father—and many of the elders—shared Levi's opinion that a warrior was a danger to our village, but you knew Connor could be trusted."

John gave a small chuckle and folded his hands in his lap. "I believe that a man is more than his occupation."

"And you were right about Connor. So does Mercer share only Connor's occupation, or his good nature as well?"

John scratched his bearded cheek. "That I cannot say. My daughter is quarantined with

Mr. Mercer for the survival of the entire village, so I have to trust Connor's opinion."

"And what is Connor's opinion of him?"

John leaned back in his chair and turned his head to look out the window. He did not speak for a moment and simply stared outside. Everett had never seen the overseer take so long to respond. Finally, John looked back at Everett and lowered his chin. "How is your mother?"

Surprised by the change of subject, Everett straightened his spine. "She is grieving. She says she needs time to get used to her life as a widow."

John nodded. "I will pay her a visit tomorrow."

Everett was not there to talk about his mother or their grief. He was there because he was worried about Bethany. He put a hand on the table. "John, I hope you don't think I'm out of line, but I love Bethany and she is locked in there with a man we don't know. I want to know she's safe. I want her out of there."

"As do I, son." John leveled his gaze on Everett. "Connor believes Mr. Mercer is a good man. They only had a professional relationship, but Connor says Mercer is intelligent and focused. He also says Mercer had a reputation for enjoying things in life that I would not approve of…" John paused while he ran his finger down the worn pages of his Bible. "But there are men in my own village who enjoy things I do not approve of. That does not mean they would harm a young woman."

Hearing his worst fear mentioned out loud ignited Everett's anger. He stood with such rapid movement his chair screeched across the floor behind him. "My father is dead and I have a farm to manage and all I can think about is Bethany in that cottage with a strange man. He almost killed her with that disease and now—"

"Sit down, son." John tapped his forefinger on the table in quick thumps.

Everett obeyed and waited for John to scold him for impatience. John said nothing and the silence made Everett feel childish. He dropped his head into his hands. "I'm afraid I missed my chance with Bethany."

When John did not respond, Everett drew his head away from his hands and looked at the overseer. John's blue eyes were focused on him with a kind but intense gaze. Everett rubbed his sweaty palms on his pants. "I'm in love with your daughter. I have been for years and I want to marry her. I knew your rule for your daughters and I planned on asking for your blessing when she turned eighteen. But then she said she wasn't ready to court, so I waited… and now I'm afraid I missed my chance."

John blew out a breath. "Everett, you are the only man in this village to whom I would give my blessing without hesitation. However," John held up a finger as he spoke. "Bethany has not given any indication that she is aware of your feelings for her. I could be wrong. Even though she seems to express her every emotion, she often keeps deeper matters to herself. Does she know you want to court her?"

"I honestly don't know."

John gave Everett's knee a hearty pat then stood. "You have my blessing, but I suggest you approach her slowly. Let her know how you feel and then give her time. I know her illness gave you a sense of urgency, but I will not give my consent to any other man, so there really is no hurry."

Everett rose and stuck his hand out, his fear somewhat allayed. "Thank you, John."

As Everett left the Colburn house, he walked to the road with a sense of approval but not the sense of peace he sought. He turned to look back at the cottage and saw warm light glowing through the curtain in the upstairs window. Desperate to speak to Bethany, he picked up a clump of dirt and walked to the cottage. With his chin lifted high toward the closed window, he threw the dirt clump. It thudded against the glass and fell to bits on the ground close to the cottage. He waited and watched for any sign of movement, but there was only the faint flicker of the firelight in the room behind the curtain. He picked up another clump and chucked it at the window. A shadow darkened the window, and then the curtain moved and Bethany appeared. When she looked down at Everett and smiled, he felt a surge in his chest.

Bethany raised the sash window and leaned her folded arms on the sill. "I am so glad to see you."

Everett wanted to respond but was suddenly without words.

Bethany angled her head. "What? Do I look terrible?"

"No, Beth, no. You look beautiful." He wanted to pour his heart out to her from right there—twelve feet below her—where he stood ankle deep in dewy grass. He swallowed the nonsensical romantic babble that waited on his tongue. "I'm so glad you recovered. I have been worried about you."

"It was horrible. I truly thought I was going to die. Connor said he thought it was close too. Now I'm fine, but I'm stuck up here for five more days." She looked at her fingernails. It made Everett imagine the pigment stains that were usually around their edges. He wondered if the discoloration had faded since she had been away from work for several days. She looked back down at him. "I'm so sorry I missed the funeral. Are you all right?"

"No, but I will be."

"Is your mother all right?"

"No, but she will be too."

Bethany smiled. "I've been thinking a lot about when we were children. I loved going to your family's property. Your father would take me to the barn and let me feed the bottle lambs."

"As soon as this is over, you can come to the farm as much as you like."

Bethany nodded and combed her fingers through her loose waves. "I miss him."

"So do I."

"He always said I was kind of like the lambs."

"He was right." He thought she was every bit as naïve as every lamb he had ever cared for. "Bethany, what is Mercer like?"

Her eyebrows raised a degree. "Justin? He has dark hair and skin and really straight teeth. He talks like Connor and he says a lot of technical things too."

"No. I want to know what he is like as a man— how does he treat you."

"Oh, fine, I guess. He doesn't talk to me when Connor is around. Besides, Connor said I have to stay up here, so I just draw all the time. I'm so bored in here. I want to go back to the pottery before it's too cold."

It was not the answer Everett wanted, but as long as Mercer was keeping to himself, he could let it rest. "What have you been drawing?"

Bethany shrugged. "Everything I can think of. I just drew a new design I might try on a dish set."

"Show me."

"You won't be able to see the detail from down there." A quick smile lit her face and she held up a finger. "Wait a minute. I have an idea."

Bethany disappeared inside the room and Everett stretched his tired neck while he waited. He heard paper crinkling inside the room, then her arm appeared in the window. She released a piece of paper folded into a peculiar, pointed shape. The white paper sailed through the air like a bird and circled overhead before it landed in the grass behind his feet. He glanced up at Bethany, then he stepped back and picked up the folded paper. "Clever."

"It's called a paper airplane. Justin taught me."

Jealousy burned inside Everett's chest, but he tried not to show it as he unfolded the paper and examined Bethany's design. Though he recognized her artistic style in the flowering vine scrolled along the page, the lines had distinct angles foreign to her usual work. He traced the fold lines in the paper with his forefinger and he wondered if Mercer's influence went beyond paper airplanes. "It's different."

"You don't like it, do you?"

"I like it just fine," Everett lied. "Does Mercer go up to your room?"

"Pardon?"

He cleared his throat, but it did little to tamp his anger. "When did he teach you to fold paper like an airplane?"

"I don't know—the other day. Look, Everett, I know you are worried about me—just like my father and Levi are—but I'm fine. Justin apologized for getting me sick and I forgave him. You all will have to forgive him too. You just haven't met him yet, so it makes you worry about me, but he's nice, really. You will like him once you get to know him."

Everett realized John was right: Bethany had no idea how he felt about her. She thought he wanted to protect her like the other men in her life. And he did, but the other men in her life were related to her; his feelings for her were much different. He would not stand in the yard and declare his feelings for the woman he loved as she leaned out a window. He would wait until he could stand close to her and touch her and watch the light in her eyes as he told her how much she meant to him.

Everett held up the paper. "May I keep this?"

Bethany smiled. "You may. Will you come visit me again?"

"I will." Everett thought of all the work that waited for him at the farm—his farm. "It will be a few days, but I will come back."

* * *

Bethany buttoned the front of an old flannel nightshirt and unwrapped the towel from her wet hair. Her damp waves fell past the shirt's tattered collar as she leaned over the sink to wipe steam from the mirror. Though late at night, she did not want to go to bed. After a week of being stuck upstairs of the cottage, she was tired of being indoors, tired of being alone, and tired of wearing old clothes from the rag pile. Though she normally loathed housework, she was looking forward to the cleaning and sanitizing Connor said they would have to do to the cottage on the last day of quarantine. She glanced down at the ugly nightshirt and felt especially thrilled with the plan to burn the old clothes she had been forced to wear.

As Bethany opened the washroom door, she wondered what Justin was doing downstairs. He had seemed interested in her on the first day of quarantine, but then Connor had said something to him. Though Bethany had strained to hear, she did not know what was said, but Justin had not called her to the door since. He only came upstairs to use the washroom when Connor was in the cottage, and he rarely said more than hello when he passed through her room. Though Connor was trying to protect her, she had no one else to talk to and she doubted Justin was still infectious.

Bethany glanced around the quiet bedroom. It felt late. The only clock in the cottage was in the office downstairs. She walked to the door and cracked it—hoping to hear if Justin was still up—and heard the repetitive creak of the floorboards followed by a gush of breath. Curious, she crept down the first few steps then knelt to peer between the balusters. Justin was splayed, arms spread wide, pushing himself up from the floor. He lowered his straight body close to the floor, and then the muscles in his shirtless back tightened as he pushed up again. Bethany sat on the stair and tucked the hem of her nightshirt around her long legs as she watched him.

Justin continued exercising and did not look up. "Do you like what you see?" he asked.

"I'm sorry for staring. I only wondered what the time was."

He pushed his body away from the floor one last time then stood. The faint light coming from the gray leaf log that burned in the fireplace highlighted one side of his face and body. The skin on the left side of his chest was marked with a dark symbol. It looked like a drawing of wings with something between them. Justin's chest rose and fell with heavy breath as he glanced at the round mechanism strapped to his wrist. "It's eleven twenty-three."

Bethany peeled her eyes away from the mark on his chest and pointed to the clock on the bookshelf beside Lydia's medical supply cabinet. "That says half past twelve."

"Your village probably calibrates with the sun. It's actually GMT minus one here." He stepped closer to the staircase then stopped and grinned. A bead of sweat rolled down his whiskered jaw. "I'm glad you finally came downstairs."

Bethany smiled back and looked at the clock on his wrist. The mechanism was as strange and foreign to her as he was. After being under the same roof for a week he should feel familiar, yet when she studied him, her mind filled with questions.

He lifted his forearm. "Haven't seen a watch like this before, have you?"

When she shook her head, he turned his arm and worked a buckle on the underside of his wrist. He removed the rubber watchband and stepped close to the staircase as he held it out. She reached through the balusters to take the watch then remembered what happened the first time she touched him. When she pulled her hand back, Justin angled his head. "What's the matter?"

"I'm sorry, I just don't want to get sick again."

"Don't worry—that's over. I'm completely healed. The gray leaf took care of it." He held the watch closer and nodded when she took it. "It's cool, huh?"

Bethany examined the strange timepiece. The clock's hands seemed to glow in the dim light of the room. The band was smooth and still warm from his body heat. She touched the buttons on either side of the clock's outer ring. "What are these?"

Justin leaned against the staircase; his face was mere inches from hers. She stared at the watch but could feel him looking at her. He reached his hand through the balusters and touched the buttons on the watch. "These two set the time and date, this is the countdown timer, and that is the backlight." He slid the watch out of her hand.

Bethany's gaze followed the watch as he strapped it back around his wrist. Her eyes trailed up to the black mark on his chest. She could see more detail now that he was close: the lines of the feathers, the shield between the wings, and the anchors below the shield. "Did you draw that on yourself?"

"No, it's a tattoo."

"Oh. I've never seen one before. Will it wash off?"

Justin rubbed a palm across the mark as if to prove its permanence. "No. A tattoo artist injects ink under the skin with needles."

"What does the symbol mean?"

He glanced at the tattoo then kept his chin low as he looked back at her. "It's the naval flight officer insignia."

Connor was a naval aviator but his skin was unmarked. Bethany asked, "Why do you have it?"

Justin leaned against the edge of Lydia's desk. His eyes cast downward. "I worked so hard during flight training that when I finally got my wings of gold, I swore I would never take them off. That wasn't practical, so I figured if I got the symbol tattooed over my heart, I would never forget what mattered most to me— wings."

"Wings matter most to you... out of everything in life?"

"Yes."

"Still? Even after what happened and not flying for three years?"

Justin didn't answer. Bethany followed the lines of the tattoo with her eyes. She remembered when she first met Justin and how he had laid her hand over his heart—over that mark. He had said he spent three years trying to find the Land, but now he said wings mattered more than everything. Bethany wrapped her arms around her knees. "Would you go back to flying if you could?"

Justin looked her in the eye. "In a heartbeat."

"When Connor first arrived, he tried to find a way to leave the Land but couldn't."

"That's bull. There's always a way out."

Bethany thought of the fierce ocean currents that ripped close to the shore of the Land. Those churning currents had taken the lives of two of her classmates when she was fifteen. The idea of another person trying to leave the Land made her feel sick. She put her hand around one of the balusters. "Are you going to try to go back to your ship?"

"I don't know yet." Justin looked at the door and then back at her. He leaned close and lowered his voice. "I wanted to find this land so badly, but now that I know the cure for the disease, I want to get some of that gray leaf medicine back to my ship. A buddy of mine is sick—he may be dead by now. The other men onboard are all sick too. If I could get the medicine to them, something good could come of all this."

"Connor says the atmosphere keeps the Land hidden and—"

"Hidden and impenetrable are two different things. If I got in, I can get out. But since I was unconscious when I arrived, I have no idea how far away my ship is. Connor said he took an old telescope out to the shore today and looked, but he couldn't see anything. Maybe I'll wire a coconut radio and try to call the ship from here."

"A what?"

"Nothing." Justin grinned. "It was a joke."

Bethany smiled back even though she did not understand. She liked him and felt a twinge of disappointment at the thought of him leaving, but she understood his desire to get medicine to his friends. Her finger traced the beveled line of the baluster. "Are you going to leave as soon as the quarantine is over?"

"I don't know."

"If you are going to try at all, shouldn't you go before your friends are dead?"

Justin crossed his arms over his bare chest. "You ask a lot of questions."

Bethany drew her head away from the balusters. "I'm sorry if I'm annoying. I'm just bored with being stuck in this place."

"Me too." He dropped his hands to the desk and a slow grin reached his eyes. "We don't have to be bored, you know. There are things we could do to entertain ourselves. I know one thing I'd really like to do."

Bethany glanced around the room then her eyes settled on a stack of the founders' books on the desk beside Justin. "I'm tired of drawing and there is nothing else to do in here but read." She pointed at the books. "Connor keeps bringing me books."

Justin's brow furrowed. "That's not exactly what I meant." He chuckled. "Yeah, he keeps bringing me these old journals from your founders. He says if I'm going to live here, I need to learn about your society."

"Have you read any of them?"

"Only a couple. I don't know if it's because these journals are a hundred years old or what, but this place seems pretty uptight. I can see why Connor likes it—he always seemed like the churchy type. He probably fit right in here, didn't he?"

"I guess. It seems like so long ago, but I remember at first people were suspicious of him—especially my brother Levi—but then Connor wanted to help keep the Land hidden from the outside world and everyone saw how sincerely he cared."

"How sincerely he cared," Justin repeated and shook his head. He stepped away from the desk and paced the office floor then turned and ran a hand over his short hair. "Yeah, I would've done the same thing. I would've tried to keep this safe, beautiful place to myself too. Clean water, miraculous medicine, gullible women—I would've done the same thing. Only I wouldn't be able to play along with all the prudish rules for as long as he has."

Bethany heard the change in Justin's voice and wondered why he sounded perturbed. She tried to sense his emotions, but he gave such conflicting signals she could not read him. "I know you've been stuck in here for a week, but once you see the village and meet people, you will probably like it here."

"Bethany—" Justin rubbed the back of his neck as he slowly stepped back to the stairs. His pants were slung low on his hips and she watched the lines of his body as he moved.

When he reached the stairs, he rested his forearms against the balusters and leaned close to her. "So far you are the only thing I like about this place." He looked at her lips. He had said he liked her and she sensed his attraction. They were alone and it was late—Connor wouldn't come in. No one would ever know. Part of her wanted everyone to know. All the young women in the village would be intrigued with Justin when they saw him, but he liked her first.

She held her breath and waited for him to move. Justin glanced at the door then pushed away from the stairs. "Go to bed, Bethany." He turned and stepped to the cot on the other side of the office.

She watched him and released the breath she had held. "Good night, Justin," she said as she stood and walked back up to her prison.

# Chapter Seven

Bethany glanced in the mirror of Lydia's old dressing table and then back at her unfinished sketch. A spare graphite pencil rolled to the edge of her temporary desk and she stopped it with her elbow. Connor's footsteps echoed up the stairway. She glanced at him as he walked into the room, then she returned her attention to the face on the page.

Connor lifted a plate of half-eaten food from the side of the dressing table. "Are you finished with this?"

"Yes, thank you."

"Nice sketch." He hovered over her while she penciled in the iris of an eye. She intentionally left a spot of white to capture a light she barely remembered.

Connor pointed to the page. "Who is it? Adeline?"

"No, it's my mother. At least it's supposed to be. I don't remember her features very well." She pulled her pencil away from the sketch and looked at the face staring back from the page. "I miss my family."

"Only one more night to go, Beth. You can do it." He rubbed a palm across her shoulder. "You'll be back in the house tomorrow morning."

"I can't wait to get out of here."

Connor motioned to the plate in his hand. "Me too. Get some sleep. Tomorrow morning we'll clean this place, burn the rags, and be done with it." He gave her a sympathetic grin before he walked back down the steps.

"Thank goodness," Bethany mumbled as she tossed her pencil onto the dressing table. She stood and stretched her arms overhead. One last night in quarantine—Connor was right— she could do it. Glancing around the messy room, she decided to start gathering her things to make the cleaning go faster in the morning. As she packed her satchel, she heard Connor and Justin speaking downstairs. Last night when Justin leaned against the stair rail, shirtless, she thought he might be intrigued with her. But his flirtatious interest had turned into abrupt dismissal. Curious as to what might be said, Bethany pushed back a tangle of bed sheets and sat on the edge of the mattress as she listened to the low murmur of the men's voices downstairs. Connor spoke too quietly for her to understand his words. She wanted to sneak to the door and listen, but they would hear the floorboards creak with her steps. She stayed on the bed and strained to decipher their conversation. Justin mentioned her name.

"No, she's too young for you," Connor said. "She just turned eighteen."

"That's legal."

"You're thirty."

"Not for two more months."

"Still," Connor insisted, "she is not your type."

"Sure she is—she's eighteen," Justin chuckled. Bethany did not know why he found that funny, but she liked the sound of his laugh.

"Things are different here. These people have old fashioned values and everything moves at a slower pace." Connor raised his volume then lowered it again. "The women here are different from the women you're used to."

"Oh, yeah? Are they all as tractable as Bethany? Cause I could get used to that."

"Tractable? No, most of the women here are strong and independent. Bethany is too in her own way. The men in her life are the leaders in this community. That's all she has known, so she is trusting—probably too trusting—of men. But don't let that give you any ideas. She may be young and naïve, but we are protective of her."

Bethany ran her fingers through her knotted hair as she sat on the bed. She felt flattered by every word Justin said about her. Every time he said her name she wanted to giggle but proudly considered herself mature for holding it in. Her fingers caught a particularly stubborn knot and it stung her scalp. She worked at the knot as she listened for more.

"Lydia says you're free to go tomorrow." Connor's voice returned to its regular volume. "So long as no symptoms return before then."

"Yeah, fine, whatever," Justin replied. Bethany desperately wanted them to go back to talking about her.

"What are you going to do?" Connor asked.

"I don't know yet. Volt was going to send a message to the navy about the icebreaker as soon as he had the American communications online."

"Do you think he's done it already?"

"I've been here ten days. If he didn't send it yet, he's probably dead."

Bethany wondered if Justin was going to mention his desire to take gray leaf medicine to the sick men on his ship, but he only spoke of communications and technical things. She wondered if Connor was going to mention the old airplane she had found below the bluffs, but he did not. She lifted a comb and listened to the men downstairs as she untangled her hair, but her name was not mentioned again.

* * *

Bethany lay in bed staring at the moon through the window. As she watched its bright, oval shape trek across the sky, she imagined Justin downstairs on their last night quarantined together. Though eager to leave the cottage, Bethany felt a sudden wave of sadness. It seemed wrong to grow sentimental of time spent imprisoned. Yet no matter which angle she considered the experience from— frightening, boring, horrific, lonely—she was determined to enjoy the final hours. She climbed out of bed and felt the heat of the gray leaf log as her bare feet passed in front of the grate in the wall. Straightening her tattered nightgown, she opened the bedroom door and peeked downstairs. The lantern on Lydia's desk was out, and the only light came from the glow of the log burning in the downstairs fireplace. She listened for movement, and when she heard nothing, she assumed Justin was asleep. Overcome with curiosity, she crept down the stairs and stopped when she saw him.

Justin was sitting on the edge of the cot with his thumb holding his place in an old book. He raised a brow and grinned when their eyes met. Then he clapped the book shut. "I was hoping you'd come see me tonight."

"Really?"

"Of course."

She almost giggled but only ran her fingers through her hair and considered herself womanly for being able to control her gestures. As Justin stood and tossed the book onto the cot, Bethany sat on the steps. She expected him to walk to the side of the stairs and look at her through the balusters as he had the night before. Instead, he rounded the newel post and rested his hand atop it as he looked her. She smiled and scooted to the edge of the step, hoping he would sit beside her.

Justin's gaze moved across her nightgown then back to her face. He lifted his chin. "Now you look like a peasant girl."

Bethany glanced down at the old nightgown and groaned. "I know. I can't believe we have to wear clothes out of the rag pile, but it all has to be burned tomorrow anyway."

"We?" Justin lifted the collar on the loose button-front shirt he wore. "Is this out of your family's rag pile too?"

"Yes, I believe that was my brother's shirt years ago." Bethany smiled. "You're quite the peasant yourself."

"Oh great." Justin chuckled. "So what should a couple of peasants do to make the most of their last night locked in the village medical cottage?"

He sat beside Bethany on the step and turned to face her. She felt an exhilarating mix of hope and doubt as she studied his features; she liked him and could love him, if she had the smallest confirmation that he loved her. The faint lines in the tanned skin of his forehead attested to his age, but that only meant he had more experience and wisdom than her and could take care of her—if he wanted to. She saw her reflection in his dark eyes and wondered what she looked like to him. He might find her a pleasing woman to be adored or just an importunate child to be dismissed. One edge of his mouth curved up as he grinned, and she felt desperate to know what he was thinking. More than that, she wanted to know what he was feeling. The emotions she sensed in him were a muddled mixture that provided no insight. She wanted him to tell her again about liking her voice and she wanted to be kissed and she wanted to be loved. He may leave the Land tomorrow and she may never see him again, but if by some chance this charming and mysterious stranger had fallen in love with her, she could convince him to stay. They could build a home and have a family and her father would know exactly what type of work in the Land would suit Justin. She would be the envy of the village women and she could captivate the young girls with her stories of being loved. But as much as she wanted to love him, she did not really know him. And as much as she wanted to be loved by him, he did not really know her. Though his mysterious past was undeniably attractive, it also seemed frightening. Questions shrouded Bethany's fantasy. She drew her head back a degree. "I just realized I know very little about you."

Justin's shoulders lifted in a slight shrug. "What's to know?"

"Where you are from, for instance, and—"

"The States."

"I meant your family and your village and what your childhood was like."

He sighed and looked away. "That doesn't matter."

"It does to me. Do you have family in America?"

He put his arm over the stair behind her shoulders then lowered his voice. "Let's just enjoy tonight, okay?"

"Okay," Bethany repeated then bit her lip. He did not want questions and she did not want to be found annoying. She wanted to talk but remained silent. Maybe she should have stayed upstairs. Ambivalent, she lifted her hands then mindlessly laid them on her thighs. "I'm sorry. I don't know why I came down here."

Justin angled his body toward her. He began to trace around her hand. His finger casually grazed her leg while he outlined her hand. "I think you do."

She watched his hand as it floated above hers. His cuffed sleeve left his forearm exposed and bluish-green points of light glowed on the watch at his wrist. Her gaze followed his arm to his chest then she remembered the tattoo beneath his shirt. He was right: she knew why she was down there—she wanted attention and affection. But as his fingers trailed along the skin of her leg, she realized the attention he was willing to give her skipped a few steps that she longed for. She moved her hand out from under his and began to inspect the silver charm dangling from her bracelet. "I just wanted to talk."

Justin released a long breath. He glanced at his watch then looked back at her. "Fine. Talk."

* * *

Everett waited while Connor swirled the water in his glass. He felt both eager and reluctant to hear the report. Connor's mood always shifted when he spoke of the outside world, of the war he escaped, or of the possibility of anyone finding the Land. Everett glanced across the Colburns' kitchen table at John and Levi. They too were watching Connor as they waited for his response.

Connor set his water glass on the table. "Mercer says he doesn't know yet if he will try to leave, but the Land is not what he expected. He said he knew I survived the crash and he felt that the people we were fighting for abandoned me. Then they did the same thing to him after the communications breakdown when they left him in Antarctica. For three years he has fantasized about what it would be like to find the Land. I think it was a coping mechanism after all that he went through. Then he got sick and just before he left the ship, his friend got the communications systems back online. Now that he is here, he misses his old life—and Mercer's life includes things that aren't exactly congruent with the way most people here live."

John lifted a palm. "It sounds like he needs a challenge. Hard work will take his mind off whatever he misses and give him a dose of reality. And he has been stuck in the cottage the whole time he has been here. Reading dusty journals about life is nothing like living it."

"It doesn't matter what he decides to do." Levi shook his head. "I don't trust him."

"Nor do I," Everett added.

"Don't get me wrong," Connor said, "I don't want to make him sound like some kind of criminal—he's not. People have to work hard for years to get where we were in the military and then it's a demanding life of stress and sacrifice. A lot of guys survive by having the mindset that since they work hard, they deserve to play hard. We just don't have the kind of entertainment in Good Springs that Mercer prefers."

Levi pointed a thumb at the door. "Then he should leave."

"That is up to him." John rubbed both hands across his face. "He is here now and we will help him however we can. I have called a meeting of the elders tomorrow at noon, and I expect you three to be there." Everett nodded even though he felt awkward taking his father's place among the elders. John stood from the table, "Good. Now if you will excuse me, gentlemen, it is getting late."

As John left the room, Levi shifted toward Connor. "Did you test the receiver we built?"

"Not yet." Connor lifted his water glass. "I'm still afraid that producing radio waves may get someone's attention out there."

Everett leaned forward. "What receiver?"

Connor and Levi exchanged a glance. They had a secret. Everett curled his toes inside his boots while he waited for one of the two men he most trusted to open up. "Well?" he asked. "What's going on?"

Connor set his glass on the table. "We found an old radio. It's a portable, modulated radio receiver and transmitter from the Second World War. It's over eighty years old and it still powers on. It's not receiving any radio signals from outside the Land and we couldn't know if it sends signals unless we built a separate receiver. So Levi and I have been using the wires and pieces from the satellite debris to make one."

"What are you going to do with it if it works?"

"I don't know." Connor looked toward the back door. "We have no defense here in the Land and with Mercer showing up I feel like… I should keep everything we find in case it's needed some day."

"Everything we find?" Everett repeated. "Who found the radio?"

"Bethany," Levi answered.

Everett's confusion grew. He had been busy with his father's death and with the farm, but never had he felt so left out. He frowned. "Bethany found a radio? Where?"

"In an old airplane—"

"What?" Everett stood and looked at Levi. "Is that how she got connected with Mercer? He came here in an airplane? You said he came here on a boat."

Connor put a hand on Everett's arm. "Calm down. The old plane she found has nothing to do with Mercer. It was buried in sediment below the bluffs. It has been there for decades. She was digging for minerals for pottery and found it."

Everett sat back down. "Why didn't she tell me?"

"I told her not to tell anyone," Connor explained. "It's war wreckage and I didn't want villagers getting hurt on it. Plus, we had to bury the pilot."

"The pilot?" Everett pushed a hand through his hair. "Does Bethany know about him too? How many secrets are you hiding?"

Levi poked a finger toward Everett. "It's not like that. Bethany ran home when she found the airplane, and Connor was the first person she saw. He told her not to tell anyone, but he told my father and me. We have been working with him during low tide to remove everything usable from the plane. No one else knows about it."

"It's really not that big a deal," Connor interjected, trying to ameliorate the situation. "The wings are missing from the plane, the engine is crushed, and most of the instruments are rusted. You are welcome to go see the wreckage or check out what we've salvaged. Everything usable is in the back of the barn."

Only feeling a degree better, Everett studied Levi and Connor. So they had not told him before; at least they were telling him now. "Does Mercer know?"

"No," Connor answered. "I'd need a really good reason to generate radio waves from the Land, and I have a feeling if Mercer knew about the transmitter, he'd want to use it." He leaned back in his seat and heaved a sigh. "This has been stressful on all of us. The quarantine will be over tomorrow. Let's get some rest."

The issue needed more discussion. Everett was not sure what to say, but he had more questions than answers. He waited a moment before he stood from his chair. "I want to see this radio."

"We'll show you tomorrow." Levi yawned as he took his glass to the sink. Then he glanced back at Everett. "Let's go."

Everett followed Levi to the door. Connor walked to the table and bent to blow out the lantern. Everett glanced out at the cottage and saw only the faint glow of firelight in the curtained windows. He turned back to Connor. "Are you going to check on Beth?"

Connor shook his head. "She'd be asleep by now."

Everett thought of Bethany in the cottage and imagined her in the bedroom upstairs alone and bored. He doubted she was asleep, but he closed the kitchen door and walked with Levi to the road. The cold night air made him shiver. Levi rushed ahead, but Everett kept glancing back at the cottage and the upstairs window. He wanted to see Bethany and tell her he would be waiting for her when she came out of quarantine. "I'm going to see if she's awake."

Levi stopped at the road. "Do you want me to wait?"

"No, if she's up, I want to talk to her for a while."

"Fine. I'm going home to my wife," Levi said as he walked onto the road.

Everett jogged across the grass to the side of the cottage. He picked up a clump of dirt and threw it at her window then waited. When she did not appear, he tried again. After the third clump of dirt, Connor opened the back door of the Colburn house.

"I had a feeling you'd try to wake her up." Connor stepped out the back door and rubbed his hands together. "It's freezing out here."

"She's not asleep."

Connor closed the door behind him. "How do you know?"

"I just do."

"Then why isn't she coming to the window?"

Everett looked at Connor and felt a dull knot in his gut. "She is with him."

"No." Connor shook his head. "They're asleep."

"Go check."

"Everett—"

"Please, just go check."

* * *

Bethany looked away from the blank spot of wall that she had been staring at for several minutes. "And sometimes I dream about her. Those are my favorite dreams. But I really don't remember her; I was only five when she died. I just remember what people told me about her. My father always says I'm emotionally sensitive like she was." Bethany turned her face toward Justin. Though he was sitting beside her on the stair with his arm behind her back, it was the way he listened that made her feel close to him.

The skin around his eyes creased as he grinned and reached for her hand. "You're so different from the women I've known."

She felt flattered but wondered how many women he had known; she searched his face, hoping it was a high enough number to make her the last woman he would ever want and low enough that he still had something left to give. She could ignore the matter altogether if she knew he loved her. "How am I different?"

"You are trusting and innocent." Justin's low voice hummed as he strung his words together. "Well, you're not that innocent or you wouldn't be down here right now. But you can't help being attracted to me, can you?" She felt a twinge of guilt mixed with desire. Her cheeks got warm and she looked away. Justin squeezed her hand. "You're like a—I don't know—like a lamb or something."

"I am like a lamb," she repeated, remembering how Samuel used to say that too. The memory made her miss him …and Everett. It felt like an eon had passed since she last saw Everett. Though he had talked to her once through the window, he had yet to return and she missed him. Justin let go of her hand and regained her attention. He curled his forefinger and ran his knuckle along the edge of her jaw. "Your innocence is beautiful. I know you've never been with a man before, but there is so much I could teach you. Do you trust me, Bethany?"

Her mind went blank as she watched Justin's mouth. Was he really saying what she thought he was saying? When he moved close enough to kiss, her insides tightened. Just as she parted her lips to answer him, the cottage door flew open. She jumped and pulled away from Justin, but he did not flinch.

Connor slammed the door shut. His nostrils flared as he lowered his chin. "Get upstairs, Bethany." He looked at her with eyes full of fury and distain. "Now!"

"No, Connor. We were just talking."

Connor stared at her for what felt like a torturous eternity, then his glare moved to Justin. "I told you to leave her alone."

"I don't need this," Justin huffed as he stood and marched up the stairs. When Bethany heard the washroom door slam, she dropped her face into her hands.

"I'll be sleeping in here tonight," Connor said.

Abject humiliation drenched Bethany. Wanting Connor to leave and not come back, she pulled her hands away from her face. "That is not necessary."

"Oh yes, it is. And when he gets out of the bathroom, I want you to go upstairs, close the door, and don't come out until you see daylight, understand?"

"I didn't do anything wrong."

"He's not right for you."

"Why are you acting like this?" She lifted her chin. "You are not my father."

Connor raised his eyebrows. "No, I'm not, but I can go get your father if you like." When her shoulders slumped, Connor nodded. "That's what I thought. Last I heard you're still under your father's authority and you need his permission to be alone with a man."

"I'm an adult now. Besides, that's a stupid rule."

Connor ignored her protest. "Your father trusted me to protect you. I left you alone out here because I thought you were mature enough to handle it, but I see I was wrong. Everett and Levi were right."

"I'm so tired of everyone telling me what to do. I like Justin. I don't care what you are worried about—I'm going to give Justin a chance. You can't keep us separated. We're going to spend time together once we are in the house anyway."

"He's not coming to the house tomorrow."

Bethany wondered if Justin planned to leave the Land after all. She did not want him to go. Her hand gripped the stair rail. "What do you mean?"

"Mrs. Vestal has offered for him to stay in her parents' old cabin."

"The one past the graveyard?"

"Yes."

"Why?"

"He has to stay somewhere."

"Why not with us?" Bethany asked, knowing the answer. When Connor only shook his head, her frustration grew. "Father welcomed you into the house before he knew you. He let you stay in our home when you and Lydia were courting. Why not Justin?"

Connor rubbed the back of his neck. "First of all, Lydia lived here and your dad took me out of here the minute I recovered from my injuries. I lived in the house and I played by your father's rules, which aren't stupid by the way—they are the traditions this culture is built on. I respected Lydia and didn't touch her until we were married. Justin isn't interested in courting. He won't restrain himself with you."

"Well, he is interested in me and I'm flattered."

"Don't be." Connor stepped closer and lowered his voice. "Whatever he said to make you feel special—it's part of his game. You mean nothing to him as a person. He would say the same things to any woman."

Bethany thought of how Justin praised her innocence and even said she was different from other women. Connor did not know what Justin had said; he could not understand. She shook her head. "I've been getting to know him and—"

Connor held up his hand. "Let me guess: he let you tell him all about yourself and it made you feel close to him. He gave you a few compliments and now you think he loves you. Am I close?"

Her mouth opened to answer, but the truth of Connor's summation stung too much for her to think of a response. She heard Justin at the top of the stairs and closed her mouth.

Connor looked up the stairs at Justin and then back at her. "Go to bed."

Humiliated, Bethany turned and walked up the stairs. She would obey and go upstairs, but she would not condemn Justin for not sharing their restrictive customs. As she passed Justin, she reached a hand out to touch his, but he passed without acknowledging her.

# Chapter Eight

Everett brushed the hay fragments from his sleeves as he slipped into the pew behind two rows of village elders. Though he had their approval to train for his father's position, Everett felt out of place, and it did not help that he was late to the meeting.

Levi was sitting at the opposite end of the otherwise empty pew, scowling, with his arms crossed tightly over his chest. The elders were discussing raising a new barn for a village family, but Everett doubted that was why Levi looked perturbed. He wondered if the issue of Justin Mercer had already been discussed and, if so, to what extent.

The afternoon sun had warmed the chapel, and sweat began to bead beneath Everett's shirt. He loosened the button at his neck and moved down the bench beside Levi.

"Where is Connor?" Everett whispered.

"He took Mercer to the old Vestal cabin." Levi angled his chin. "He wants to keep an eye on him for a while."

"Good." Everett kept his voice quiet. "Connor found Mercer and Bethany together last night after you went home."

Levi snapped his head toward Everett. "Doing what?"

"They were sitting on the stairs talking, but apparently they grew fond of each other during the quarantine."

Levi blew out a breath as he turned his face toward the front of the church. "I don't like that."

"Me neither," Everett mumbled as the elders' discussion about the barn raising ended. Then he leaned toward Levi. "Has anyone mentioned Mercer yet?" Levi shook his head once.

John glanced at his notes and began to address the elders. "Thanks to Connor's diligence, we have contained the illness. The gray leaf medicine worked against the bacteria, so the disease is no longer a threat. The quarantine is over and Justin Mercer will be staying in the vacant cabin owned by Mrs. Vestal. Mr. Mercer is still not sure if he will attempt to leave the Land or not, but until he decides, he must work. I spoke with Justin this morning, and he understands we all eat because we all work. He has agreed to accept whatever employment is offered. Does anyone have—"

"I will give him work." Everett stood as he declared his offer. The elders in the rows in front of him shifted in their seats and craned their necks to see him as he spoke for the first time in an official meeting.

"Very well." John raised an eyebrow but gave no other indication of the unnerving developments regarding Mercer. He scribbled a note on his paper. "I will tell Justin to report to the Foster property first thing in the morning."

Everett sat back down. He did not look directly at Levi, but he could tell Levi was looking at him.

"That was charitable of you," Levi whispered.

"It wasn't charity at all."

"Are you going to let him live long enough to regret coming here?"

"Regret it? Yes. Let him live? That I can't promise."

John pointed his pencil at Everett. "Also, Everett, many of the villagers have asked if you plan to continue your father's tradition of hosting the autumn party. Have you given that any thought?"

Everett stood again but this time with less vigor. "Yes. My mother will be organizing the party this year. Several of the village women are helping her. She has asked for extra time to prepare, so I decided we'll have the party at the end of April."

"Excellent. Thank you, Everett."

Everett sat and leaned his back against the hard pew. He looked at the front of the chapel and studied the wooden cross that hung from the vault in the ceiling. John closed the meeting with prayer, and then the men filed out of the pews toward the tall chapel doors. Everett stayed in the pew and stared at the bare cross.

John stepped away from the podium and stopped in the aisle near Everett. "You look like you have the weight of the world on your shoulders."

Everett glanced at the overseer. "My father used to say that phrase."

"That is probably where I got it." John lowered himself into the pew next to Everett. "I know you had to put in a full day of work by noon to get here today. I am pleased you came. Are James and Nicholas good workers?"

"They are."

"And you will have more help starting tomorrow—that is, if your offer was sincere."

Everett nodded. "It was sincere—self-serving, but sincere."

"Ah. I wondered." John leaned back and crossed his arms. He allowed a few moments of silence then drew a breath. "I remember when my father was no longer able to carry out his duties as overseer and it was time for me to take the position. I was trained and ready but terrified to accept my inheritance. Hannah and I had only been married a short while. I wanted to prove to her more than anyone that I could do it. I remember going home at the end of a particularly hard day and instead of showing her kindness, I lashed out at her about something trivial. She saw right through me." John gave a short chuckle. "She told me to never try to hide my insecurities from her again because I was robbing her of the opportunity to love me through a difficult time."

Everett took his eyes off the cross. "I'm sorry, but I fail to see your point."

"Whom do you most want to prove yourself to?"

"My father. I know it doesn't make sense—he is dead."

"Of course it does—he gave you a fine example and a weighty inheritance."

As much work as Everett had to do, it was not the farm that burdened him or even the fact that he had his father's reputation to live up to. He stretched his collar away from his sweaty neck. "I'm twenty years old and I'm running the largest farm in the village and declaring my decisions among the elders. I want to be a man my father would be proud of. He told me to hire men and treat them fairly. He told me to take care of my mother and sister."

"These are all things you have been helping him with since you were young. You know how to run the farm and take care of family."

Everett shook his head, recalling his father's dying wishes. "He also told me he wanted me to marry Bethany."

"Is that his wish or yours?"

"Both. It was his wish because he knew it's my greatest longing. Now she's intrigued with another man—this outsider—and though I know he will not marry her, I fear he will sully her."

John shifted in the pew. "Bethany may be naïve, but she is morally grounded. I do not think it will come to that, but if you do, the question is: would you still love her?"

Everett did not want to imagine it let alone postulate his ability to forgive. His breath burned in his dry throat and he glanced at the cross as he waited for the words to come. "I would forgive her, but I'd rather protect her from it happening in the first place." He swallowed hard and looked at John. "I miss my father a great deal and I cannot ask his advice, so I'll ask you... what should I do?"

* * *

Bethany dumped the contents of her satchel onto her bed. Having spent the morning scrubbing the cottage, she was tired of cleaning and decided to put her things away later. She looked around her bedroom, grateful finally to be back in her own space. A wooden trunk in the corner of the room caught her eye. She focused on the flowers painted around its edges and the row of dolls arranged on its top as she stepped toward the heirloom box. The dolls had gone untouched for years, aside from Lydia's occasional dusting rampage. Bethany could not recall the last time she opened the lid. She knelt on the floor and looked at each doll, trying to remember their names as she moved the toys to the floor. As she lifted the trunk's lid, Lydia stepped into the room. "Did you miss your toys, little sister?"

Though Lydia smiled when she said it, Bethany thought the question held more jest than sentiment. She did not smile back. "I'm not a child anymore."

Lydia sat on a half-size school chair that was pushed against the wall by the trunk. "That's not what I meant."

Bethany looked inside the trunk. It was full of play clothes, ribbons, toy teacups, and doll blankets—all the girl toys passed down from her three elder sisters. Levi always had his own toys; they were still in the trunk in his old room, which was now Andrew's nursery. As a child Bethany had preferred Levi's toys because they could be taken outside and played with in the dirt.

"I missed you," Lydia said.

"I missed you, too." Bethany pulled a painted conch shell from the bottom of the trunk. "Remember when I found this shell on the shore and brought it home? I wanted to paint it, but you and Adeline and Maggie all told me to leave it how it was." Dried paint flaked onto Bethany's fingers as she rubbed her hand across the shell. She chuckled and held it up. "I'm not sure what I was trying to prove. I painted an ugly design. Now I see how pretty the shell would have been unpainted. I guess that's why you all told me to leave it alone. But I enjoyed painting it at the time and that's what matters. Right?"

"With a shell—yes. With bigger matters in life— you need to listen to those who've gone before you." Lydia's maternal tone irritated Bethany's already frayed nerves. Lydia sat forward in the little chair. "Ten days… that was the longest you've ever been away from home, isn't it?" She was trying to get her to talk. When Bethany did not respond, Lydia continued. "Well, I'm glad you're back in the house and… safe."

"Justin isn't dangerous." Bethany laid the shell back inside the trunk and covered it with a heap of play clothes. "I don't know what Connor told you, but I got to know Justin and he is a good man. He's actually a lot like Connor."

"You just think that because he sounds like Connor?"

"No. You don't know him."

"Do you love him?"

Bethany wondered that herself. She liked him and—with little effort—could imagine loving him, but their connection lacked something unnamable. She picked up the old dolls from the floor and began stuffing them inside the trunk. "I don't know. Maybe. I think I could love him. He's smart and charming and has the most beautiful voice I've ever heard. And the way he looks at me when no one else is around…"

"It sounds like you're intrigued with him."

Bethany closed the lid on the trunk, satisfied that all her childish possessions were now out of sight. "So what if I am? So what if we are attracted to each other and love each other?"

Lydia stood and folded her hands. "Those are two different things. Attraction is a biological help to ensure procreation. It's an enjoyable benefit of romance, but it isn't love."

"Is this a medical lecture?" Bethany pushed away from the floor and walked back to her satchel. "You have Connor. Now another outsider has arrived—a charming and mysterious man who will no doubt intrigue every woman in the village—and he is interested in me. You should be happy for me. You had your fun, now why can't I have mine?"

Lydia stabbed her finger into the air at Bethany. "You think I'm trying to keep you from something good when I'm actually concerned you are making a bad choice."

Bethany boosted her volume. "I'm sorry I'm not perfect like you."

Lydia's eyes widened. She blinked rapidly then glanced at the door. Footsteps echoed in the hallway as Connor climbed the stairs. His brow furrowed when he rounded the landing and looked at Bethany. She wondered how much he had heard and glanced back at Lydia. The tip of Lydia's nose was red like she was about to cry. Guilt gripped Bethany's throat and she regretted what she said. She knew she should apologize in the moment, but she could not get herself to say anything.

Connor leaned a hand into the doorframe and sighed when he looked at Lydia. "The elder meeting is over, but your dad won't be home for a while." He looked back at Bethany and his scowl returned. "There's someone downstairs who wants to talk with you."

Bethany assumed he meant Justin. She controlled the beaming smile that threatened to splay across her face. "Does he have my father's permission?"

Connor glanced at Lydia then back at Bethany and grinned. "Yes, actually, he does."

* * *

Everett used the reflective glass door of a bookcase in the Colburns' parlor for a mirror and combed his hair with his fingers. His reflection blurred as he focused on the books inside the glass. The inscriptions on several leather bound volumes attested to the Colburns' long lineage of faith. It was a heritage he planned to pass to his future children, but first he had to get the woman he loved to let him court her.

Everett looked away from the books when he heard footsteps on the stairs. Bethany's fingers skimmed the handrail as she descended the steps into the parlor. Her smile faded when her eyes met Everett's. The change was subtle, but he noticed. He grinned anyway. "Were you expecting someone else?"

"I'm glad you came. I missed you." Skirting his question, Bethany reached her arms up and hugged him the way a child hugs her father. She let go quickly, but he held her for one more heartbeat. After she pulled away, she flopped onto the divan and gave her voice a dramatic inflection. "You have no idea how awful it was being trapped in that cottage for ten days. I was so bored. I wished you would have come to see me more, but I understood why you couldn't."

Everett rounded the edge of the divan and sat beside her. "I would have slept on the ground beneath your window the entire time if I could have, Beth."

"That's sweet of you to say." She shifted sideways and propped her arm on the back of the divan. Then her smile mellowed into a caring grin and her voice lowered from its ebullient tone. "And after all you've been through. This has been a hard time for you too. It didn't seem fair—our being separated when we needed each other. I wanted to go to the funeral so badly. I hated being apart from you while you were grieving."

"Don't worry. There's plenty left."

"Grief?"

Even while sitting beside the woman he loved, Everett ached from losing his father. He pressed his lips together and nodded. "We're together now. Let's focus on that."

"Do you want to talk about it?"

"About losing Father?" When she inclined her head, he watched the light hit her blue eyes. "My sweet Beth, I know you're willing to share my grief, but that's not why I came."

"Oh?"

"I thought I was going to lose you."

"But you didn't. I survived the illness. The boredom afterward turned out to be a far greater threat to my survival. I was so lonely at times, I thought it would kill me."

Everett grinned at her exaggeration. "People do not die from boredom. Besides, you had Mercer in there with you. I'm sure you enjoyed getting to know the newcomer, didn't you?"

A sullenness marked Bethany's expression. She pulled her arm off the back of the divan. "I suppose."

"I know you're fond of him." Everett had promised himself he would not ask, but the words slithered from his tongue. "Do you love him?"

"Are you asking as my friend or as an elder?"

"Are there two different answers?"

Bethany's eyes glanced to the left then back at him. "No."

"Be honest with me."

She looked at her hands. Everett watched her face as she picked at a cuticle. Finally, she glanced back up at him. Her fingers continued their nervous picking. "I don't know. And that is the truth."

Hearing her indecision was better than hearing her declare her love for another man. If she did not love Mercer, Everett still had a chance. He would fight for her. He would give her the space and the time John advised, but he would not give up. He reached his hands to hers and pulled her fidgeting fingers apart. "Do you love me?"

Bethany's eyes widened. She sat silently and left her hands under his. Then she smiled and dimples pitted her cheeks. "Of course, Everett. You've always been my dearest friend."

"I cherish our friendship too, Beth, but that's not what I meant. I asked you to be honest with me and now I am going to be honest with you." His heart hammered against the wall of his chest as her smile disappeared. He drew a deep breath. "For the past two years I planned to declare my love for you on your eighteenth birthday, but when it got close, you complained about the boys who were waiting to court you. You said you weren't ready. So I decided to give you time. Then you almost died and I was so scared I would lose you before I had a chance to tell you how I felt. I don't know if you still want more time, but if you are willing to consider Mercer, then you need to know that I love you." He left his hands piled on hers, desperate for the connection.

Bethany sat silently for a moment, then released a long breath. "I don't know what to say. I had no idea you felt that way about me. I must admit I was intrigued with you when we were in school, but then after the attack last year, I—we—changed. People have sometimes suggested that we belong together, but I had no idea you…"

Everett inched closer to her on the divan and could smell an intoxicating mixture of gray leaf oil and soap on her skin. He had to force himself to focus on their discussion. "I won't rush you. I will wait for you for however long you need. Just please promise you will tell me if you start considering another man."

She shook her head in slow and rigid movements. "I already am."

"Him?"

"Maybe. I don't know. I already told you: I don't know. I'm attracted to him and I know he is attracted to me." When Everett gave a frustrated groan, Bethany shrugged. "You told me to be honest."

"Yes, I did. I just… fine… I can wait for you to sort that out because I love you and if you do accept me, I don't want you wishing you were with someone else."

"I would never do that."

"Just please, promise me you won't spend time alone with him without your father's permission."

"Those old rules are only because people don't trust each other."

"No, they are for your protection."

Bethany angled her chin. "Would you consider marrying a woman you don't trust?"

"Of course not."

"Do you trust me?"

"I don't trust him."

Bethany drew her hands away. "That wasn't my question."

"He is experienced in things you can't imagine."

"Is my imagination so dull?"

"You are naïve and trusting—"

"First my imagination and now do you disparage my intelligence?"

"No, Beth—" Everett moaned at her captious questions.

"How about my morals? Connor and Lydia both seem to think I could be easily seduced. Do you agree with them?"

"I do but not because of a lack of morals on your part but on his." Everett stood and pushed his hand through his hair. "If Mercer is given the chance, he will take advantage of your innocence."

"He said he loves my innocence."

"Because he wants to take it away."

Bethany stood and matched Everett's tone. "You don't know him."

"I don't need to know him. He is toying with the woman I love." Everett stepped close. The tips of his fingers burned, wanting to touch her again, but he did not. "I know you, Beth. I know what you want and what you need. I know that right now, more than anything, you want to get back to the pottery yard and sink your fingers into clay. I know you are sensitive and eager to please and you see possibilities in everything, but I won't take advantage of that. I know I can trust you—you found a skeleton in an airplane and kept it a secret. Three years ago you would have blabbed that to anyone who'd listen. More importantly, I know how to love you and how to protect you. I saved your life once and I would gladly do it again. I would try to protect you from anyone and anything, but I cannot protect you from yourself."

* * *

Bethany slid her arm through her pail's handle, wedged her trowel between her teeth, and began to climb the boulders beneath the bluffs. She ignored the remnants of the old airplane's wreckage buried in the sediment nearby and gripped the next chink in the rock to climb to the top of the boulder nearest the eroded cliff. It would all be worth it if the mineral sparkling in the face of the rock were what she hoped. As she pulled herself onto the boulder's level top, she withdrew the trowel from her mouth and spit the dirt from her lips. The sparkle in the cliff face was within arm's reach, but she would have to work quickly if she were to return the way she came.

She set her pail between her feet on the boulder and glanced back at the ocean. The tide was already changing. Determined to get a sample of the sparking minerals before she had to climb back down, she planted one palm on the cliff and scratched its surface with her trowel. Loose soil sprinkled her face. She wiped her brow with her sleeve and continued working. After a second scraping, she loosened a chunk of the quartz. Tucking the trowel beneath her arm, she rubbed the crystal with the fabric of her skirt. As she examined the gleaming stone she heard someone above the cliff. "Hello?" she called out.

"Bethany?" Everett stepped to the edge and looked down at her. "What are you doing down there?"

"I found some nice chunks of quartz." She held up the crystal and then scowled at him. "What are you doing here?"

"I came to look at the airplane wreckage, but when I saw the tide was quickly changing, I decided not to." He squatted between the tussock grass on the cliff. "Did you climb down there?"

"No. I climbed up here. I was down below getting minerals to make black glaze and I saw this quartz sparkling in the sunlight. What girl could resist?" She smiled as she dropped the crystal into her pail and reached her trowel up to loosen another chunk.

Everett chuckled. "Actually, I think most girls would resist scaling a cliff face for a bit of quartz, but you aren't like most girls."

Though focused on chipping away the rock, she liked what he said. "Why haven't you come to see me this week?"

"Give me your tools. You need to climb up here."

"Be patient. I've almost got it." She raised her voice over the sound of the encroaching waves as she chipped away the loose sediment. "I asked you a question."

"The tide is coming."

"Not yet," she replied as she pulled another lump of quartz from the rock. Its clear surface glimmered as it captured the light. "It's beautiful, isn't it?"

"Beth?"

"Hm?"

"Look down."

Bethany glanced back, expecting to see the sand between the boulders and the ocean, but the water was now filling the caves and lapping at the cliff. The fright of seeing the water swirl around the rocks below ruined the excitement of her happy find. "Oh dear. I don't want the tide to come in yet."

"The sea does not do what you want it to." He lay on his chest on the cliff's edge and reached his arm down to her. She shook her head, refusing his help. He grinned. "What? You don't want to be rescued?"

"Not while you are wearing that smirk." A wave sprayed her boots as she picked up her pail and held it up to him. His fingers skimmed hers as he took her tools. She wanted his help, but did not want to admit it. "I'm capable of climbing up there myself, you know."

Everett flung her tools behind him and stretched both arms down. "I suggest you choose another time to prove your self-sufficiency."

Water soaked the back of her skirt. "Fine." Ignoring the urge to pout, she reached up and locked wrists with him as her feet found tiny clefts in the rock face. "You could hardly call this a rescue since I'm—" The rock crumbled beneath her foot, but Everett quickly pulled her over the cliff. With a flex of his muscles he had saved her once again. She crawled onto the grass and laughed.

Everett rolled onto his back and laughed too. When his laughter died out, he looked at her. "You were saying?"

In playful offense, Bethany lifted a hand to smack his shoulder, but he took her hand and held it. She lay beside him, inches from the edge of the cliff, safe on the grassy bluff while the waves broke against the boulders below.

Everett loosened his grip on her hand but did not let go. "Actually, that was a close one."

"Then why are we laughing?"

His smile relaxed into a soft grin. "Because it's you and me and that is what we do."

"It is what we used to do."

"It has been a while." Lying beside her, Everett turned his face to the sky. "We've both been through so much."

She looked up too. The blue of the unblemished afternoon sky stretched to the edges of her vision. Its expanse made her feel unbalanced. Needing something grounded to focus on, she turned her head toward Everett. "I've missed you."

"I've been trying to give you the time you need to make your choice." He pulled his gaze away from the sky and looked at her. "And I've missed you too."

"I don't just mean this past week—I mean for a while now," she said. The way Everett watched her as he listened made her want to vocalize her every thought, uncensored. He would let her do so and think no less of her for it. He would not tell her to stop talking or demean her opinions or try to change the subject if she said something that made him uncomfortable. He had said he knew her and loved her, but she felt a distance between them and could not ignore it any longer. "After Mandy and I were attacked last year, you and I both changed. We don't laugh together like we used to. Everything seems so serious between us now."

"Perhaps we simply grew up."

"Perhaps." She thought about it for a moment. "No, going through that changed us somehow. I know it made you protective of me—like Levi and Connor are."

"Yes, but I am not your brother."

"I know," she quickly replied. In perfect comfort, she left her hand in his as they lay on the sunlit grass. She was content beside him, safe and loved. He wanted more from her, but he would not try to pressure or persuade her.

He wanted to court her, and the prospect grew more appealing to her every day. The familiarity of their lifelong friendship had always enabled her to tell him the things she could tell no one else. She wondered if that still held true. Deciding to test him, she looked back at the expansive blue above. "When the illness overtook me, I thought I was dying, and for a moment, I wanted to. I knew it would hurt at first, but then it would be peaceful and I would never feel pain again. Death seemed so appealing." Everett did not reply, but she could feel him looking at her, so she continued. "I knew if I died, I would get to see my mother, and for a moment I wanted that more than I wanted to live." She glanced at him then. He did not appear concerned or judgmental, but only watched her, listening just as he always had. "I could never tell that to anyone else. I can't imagine what people would think if I told them I thought I was going to die and I liked it. I've always been able to trust you with my deepest secrets."

"Me too, Beth. And why do you think that is?"

"I don't know."

He released her hand and played with the silver bracelet around her wrist. "Well, maybe your heart knows something you don't."

Everett looked back at the sky. From the side, Bethany studied the contours of his face, the stubble along his jaw, the dark swoop of his eyebrow. She would sketch his profile later, so that no matter what happened, she would always remember this moment. "This feels more real than the entire ten days I spent in quarantine."

A grin creased Everett's face but he did not look at her. His chest rose as he drew a deep breath. "That should count for something."

Bethany leaned her cheek against his shoulder. "That counts for everything."

# Chapter Nine

Bethany shivered as she drew the crocheted edges of her woolen shawl close to her chin. The cold air swirled fallen leaves on the road behind the wagon while her father drove them to the Foster farm. The wooden crate she used for a seat rattled with every bump in the road. Her favorite red dress would probably be filled with splinters before she even made it to the annual autumn party. She picked at her cuticles, anxious to see Everett.

Lydia was sitting near Bethany's feet on the floor of the wagon. Baby Andrew—wrapped snuggly in his light blue blanket—cooed with contentment in Lydia's arms. Connor was perched on the side of the wagon with one hand behind Lydia's back as if she were the one in danger of falling out. Bethany glanced at her father while he drove the wagon onto the Fosters' property. It saddened her to see him alone on the front bench; though it was village custom for an entire household to arrive at a party together, Isabella was too weary to go out in the cold.

The sun sank behind a silver bank of clouds to the west and took with it the last light of day. John pulled the wagon around the back of the Fosters' massive barn and parked beside the other wagons. Connor jumped down from the side and met Lydia at the back of the wagon. He took the baby then offered Lydia his free hand and helped her down. Bethany stood and brushed the splinters from her dress.

John stepped to the back of the wagon and offered her his hand. "I guess it is just you and me representing my family tonight. Shall we greet the host?"

"It is the custom." Bethany smiled as she took her father's arm and started walking beside him through the dark to the outdoor gathering.

"There he is." John pointed as they walked around to the front of the open barn. "He already has a line of villagers waiting to greet him. I guess we are late."

Bethany still thought of the property as belonging to Samuel. The warm light from myriad lanterns flowed out of the barn and lit the crowd that waited to speak to Everett. The certainty of Samuel's death and Everett's new position hit her at once. Bethany stopped walking. "It's Everett."

"Of course it is." John glanced at her. "You sound surprised."

"I don't know why, but I was expecting to see Samuel."

"Since he died while you were in quarantine and you missed the funeral, you did not have proper closure like the rest of us." John inclined his head. "Bethany, you should know that Everett has stepped into his father's position with authority and dignity. He is doing a fine job of managing his affairs and he deserves everyone's respect—including yours."

Everett greeted his guests with confident grace. He shook a village elder's hand and nodded as he listened to whatever the man was saying. At first Bethany found it odd for Everett to act as if he were comfortably one of the adults. Then the truth set in: he was not only one of them but also becoming a leader among them. And he wanted her by his side. Yet she was not one of the adults—at least she did not feel like one of them. In her mind, she was still a child. The voice of her thoughts still sounded like a child's voice. But as she watched Everett, she realized they were no longer children. He was a man, a capable leader, and would make an excellent husband. Bethany wrapped her arms around her grown body. She was a woman now and—no matter how childlike she felt on the inside—the eternally young voice of her mind was no match for the truth of the advancement of time.

John nudged her. "You look confounded."

"I'm not surprised or confused by what you said, it's just that… I just realized we are no longer children."

"Well, it is about time you did." John chuckled. He gave her arm a gentle tug and they continued walking to the line. "You will find it freeing to acknowledge life as it actually is."

Nervous, Bethany felt the silver charm on the bracelet at her wrist as she waited with her father in the line. She watched Everett while the people in front of her moved away. When his gaze landed on her, his cool grin of propriety stretched into a happy smile. He turned his head toward John, but left his focus on Bethany until the last second. "Good evening and welcome, Mr. Colburn."

"Thank you, Mr. Foster." John thrust his hand out and shook Everett's.

Everett looked at Bethany and his jovial smile returned. "Miss Colburn, I'm pleased to see you."

Bethany wanted to throw her arms around his neck and hug him and tell him to stop being so formal, but it was his job tonight and his honor was at stake. And she was no longer a child. Suddenly, her childish urge seemed distasteful. She lifted her hand to Everett, leaving her wrist bent in the most feminine way possible. "Thank you, Mr. Foster."

Everett took her hand and gave it a polite squeeze. "It's my pleasure." Then he chuckled and for a moment she saw the boy who sat beside her in class—the boy she shared secret jokes and meaningful glances with. His laugh waned and his eyes became serious, drawing her back into the present. As the sound of a violin began, he pointed an open palm toward the barn. "I hope you enjoy yourself this evening."

John moved away and Bethany walked to the barn. When her father began his usual round of greetings through the crowd, she glanced back at Everett. He was talking to Mr. and Mrs. Ashton but watching her. Though it had been comforting to hear her father's approbation of Everett, seeing him on his property, greeting his guests, and watching her with longing had a powerful effect Bethany did not anticipate. She felt a twinge of pleasure and imagined herself standing beside Everett, greeting their guests to their property. A surge of attraction, beyond what she called intrigue, sank into her with ineffable force. He was right: he knew her and loved her. She knew him and loved him too. Bethany tried to look away, but her eyes refused to move. Falling in love felt a lot like suffocating, which was fine—she would gladly forgo breathing and let this certainty of love sustain her.

Bethany smiled and wove through the crowd. As she turned to walk into the barn, Justin walked out. He stopped close to her and grinned. "Hey, beautiful."

"Hello, Justin." She smiled and glanced at his dirty work clothes. "I see you helped make the party possible."

"Not voluntarily." His expression soured.

"Oh." Bethany nodded even though she did not understand the bitterness in his tone. She looked inside the clean, empty barn. A platform in the middle was set with instruments, lanterns hung from the rafters, and benches were arranged around the expansive room. "Everything looks nice. You did a good job."

"Yeah, thanks." Justin stretched his neck. "Anyway, I was just leaving."

"Leaving? Why?"

"I'm not really welcome here." He glanced over Bethany's shoulder. "It's a shame because I'd really like to spend some time with you. You should come see me at the cabin later."

Bethany followed his line of sight to see what or who Justin was looking at while he spoke. She saw Everett scowl at Justin then glance briefly at her before he returned his attention to the guests around him. She looked back at Justin. "That would be inappropriate."

"Inappropriate? Seriously?" Justin snickered faintly. "Why? Are you dating Everett now or something?"

"A couple of weeks ago he asked me to court, and I plan to give him my answer this evening. Besides, according to our custom a woman is not supposed to go to a man's house alone."

Justin glanced again in Everett's direction then put his hand on Bethany's shoulder. He lowered his chin and looked at her the same way he did on their last night in quarantine. "You shouldn't care so much about what everyone else thinks. Forget the custom for a minute—what do you want to do?"

Bethany recognized his desire but she sensed nothing from him but disdain. She waited to see if she would feel the spark that she had felt with him in the cottage, but it never came and she was glad. She took a step back. "Thank you for the invitation, but I can't."

"Then maybe I'll have to come see you." Justin winked at her and walked away.

Bethany lingered in the open doorway of the barn. She watched Justin as he disappeared into the darkness toward the road. Then she looked at Everett. He too was watching Justin leave. Everett's visage clearly portrayed his dissatisfaction with Justin. She thought of the duality she sensed in Justin. Now that she recognized the way he dissembled, his charm was less alluring. In the light of maturity, she appreciated Everett's honest expressions. Though Bethany was flattered by having two men compete for her affection, she was relieved when Justin left the party.

As Bethany stepped into the barn, the song ended and Mandy set her violin in its case. Everett's guitar was propped against the back of the stage. Though Samuel's absence made the party feel different from those in previous years, if Mandy and Everett led the music, celebration had a chance of overcoming grief.

Roseanna whirled past the open doorway. She had a sweaty forehead and a beaming smile. "Everyone, come out and find a seat. Mr. Colburn is about to say the blessing."

After dinner Bethany dropped her shawl on a bench in the barn and clapped to the beat as she joined other dancers in the center of the room. She loved the liveliness of the jig that Mandy was playing on a new wood violin. Smiling, Bethany danced while the robust notes filled the barn. Before the song ended, a young man took her hand and danced beside her. Though he was one of the men who wanted to court her, she danced with him out of politeness. Mandy began the polka next, and the young man stayed beside her. When he looked away, Bethany took a few steps back. He glanced at the empty space where she had been and his smile vanished until he spotted her. His toothy grin returned as he stepped back beside her and took her hand again.

Skirts twirled as the couples moved in quick chasse steps around the dance floor. Bethany laughed, enjoying the comedy provided by her partner's lanky inelegance. She applauded the musicians when the music ended and then wiped her sweaty cheek with her sleeve. After thanking the young man for the dance, she began to walk to an empty bench but stopped when someone tapped her shoulder.

Another boy from school held out his hand. "May I have the next dance?"

The fresh air blowing through the doorway beckoned her, but if she were seen only dancing with one man, it may give the wrong impression. She fanned her face with her hand and mustered a courteous smile. "Yes, you may."

During the dance the two young men eyed each other with jealous glares. Bethany hoped her willingness to dance had not given the impression she was interested in courting either one. When the song ended, Mandy set her violin in its case and left the stage. Bethany swirled her hair into a twist and let the air hit her neck as she stepped away from the dancers. Everett rushed into the barn and onto the platform. He strapped his guitar over his shoulder and gave its tuning a quick check then said something to the other musicians. They nodded and began to play.

Delighted to see Everett take the stage, Bethany slipped away from the dance floor and scanned the room for a less crowded place where she could sit and watch him in peace. She heard a scuffle behind her and looked back to see her two dance partners fighting each other.

As one young man planted his fist into the other's jaw, Bethany gasped. "No!" she shouted. Levi brushed past her as he parted the crowd. When he reached them, he yanked the young men apart. With one fistful of a man's shirt and one hand around the other man's neck, Levi forcibly removed them from the dance floor.

Bethany's mouth hung open as she watched her brother haul the squabbling young men out of the barn. She took a calming breath, and then looked back at the stage. Everett gave her a wink, stomped a beat, and continued playing the song. The dancing villagers quickly filled the vacant space on the floor.

Mandy stepped beside Bethany and tugged on her elbow. "Come with me. I need some air and I think you do too."

"Thank you," Bethany shouted over the sound of the music and the clapping as Mandy hurried her to the side door of the barn. She slowed her pace once they were outside and pointed to a picnic table on the outskirts of the party.

"What do you think Levi did with those boys?" Bethany asked as she sat on the tabletop and rested her feet on the bench below.

"He probably dropped them in the dirt by the road and told them to go home." Mandy chuckled. Her laugh sounded like music. "I'm not sure which of us had the bigger thrill: me watching my husband effortlessly haul two brawling men out of the barn or you watching the two men fight over you."

Bethany laughed with Mandy then shook her head. "It was not a thrill for me. I didn't want their attention in the first place."

"Then that is where we differ. When I was your age, I loved having men compete over me." Mandy sat on the table beside Bethany and drew a long curl of her auburn hair into her fingertips. "How about the other two men who have been vying for your attention? Do you find that flattering?"

"Oh, thank goodness you said something!" Bethany let out an exaggerated sigh and shifted her body toward Mandy. "I haven't had anyone to talk to about it. When I mention it at home, it either causes hurt feelings or ends in a vehement lecture about the value of tradition."

Mandy tilted her head. "You can always talk to me. I will keep your secrets, but I can't promise not to give unbiased advice—it is my brother who has declared his love for you and is waiting kindly but anxiously for your answer."

"I know." Bethany looked across the paddock behind the noisy barn at the animals that would normally be in their stalls enjoying the quiet this time of night. A colt stood near its mother on the other side of the fence. Bethany thought of her own mother. She glanced back at Mandy. "I can sense things in people; I feel what they are feeling. My father always says it's a gift and that I'm just like my mother. It doesn't always feel like a gift. Like when I play cards with you and Levi and Connor... Levi always tells me I have to learn how to discern the other players' motives, but I just get confused when a person feels one way but acts another. I can't call anyone's bluff and it just feels unfair. At first, I was intrigued with Justin—what's not to like? He's charming and smart and comes from a world I can only imagine. When we were alone in the cottage, he would look at me and say the most alluring things." Bethany waved a hand. "Not that we did anything regrettable. We didn't. After I was back in the house, I thought about how I'd never met a man like Justin before. But when the feeling faded, I realized that even though I enjoyed his flattery, I never felt love from him. His attraction lacked affection and I'd never experienced that before."

Mandy nodded then leaned her palms on the table behind her. "Bethany, you were raised surrounded by men of integrity, so you probably assumed all men possessed that trait. But believe me, it is rare. Integrity is difficult to develop but easy to fake—at least for a while. It's the kind of pretense that cannot be sustained. Take the time to get to know a man not by what he says but by what he does, and not only when he knows he is being watched or when it benefits him. Watch what a man chooses when doing the right thing will put him at risk."

"Like when Everett saved me during the attack last year?"

"Yes, like that." Mandy took her hands off the table and brushed her palms together. "But Justin is a warrior and Connor has said their profession put them at personal risk every day, so that might not be the best example. Watch how a man behaves in less heroic moments. For example, how many times since you and Everett were teenagers have you been at our house or he at yours late at night playing cards or talking alone?"

Bethany thought back and then shook her head. "I have no idea how many times… countless."

"During any of those times alone did Everett try anything inappropriate with you?"

"No. Never."

"See—integrity." Mandy winked. "I warned you my advice might be biased."

"You're right." She chuckled at Mandy. "But my mind was already made up."

"Oh?"

"After the quarantine, I didn't see Justin again ...until tonight. I knew he was working here for Everett every day, but my father wouldn't invite him over even for dinner. And Connor didn't seem to care. He goes to Justin's cabin in the evenings, but Justin never comes to our house. I wondered if my father and Connor and Everett were in on it together, though that didn't account for why Justin doesn't go to church. Anyway, I realized that whatever I felt for him must have been a result of what I went through in quarantine. I nearly died and then I was locked up with him for days. I didn't feel anything when I saw him tonight. Those feelings of intrigue were gone."

Mandy smiled. "I'm glad to hear that, but don't feel bad for feeling the way you did during the quarantine. You went through a lot—something none of us have ever been through. Blame the boredom. Blame human nature. Blame his deceitful charm and your inexperience. Just don't blame your father and Connor and Everett for how they've handled it. Those men love you and they want to protect you."

When Mandy nudged her, she smiled. "I know. I just wish I had been prepared when Everett told me he loved me. I love him too and I would be honored to court. I wish I'd said yes."

"It doesn't hurt a man to make him wait a little."

Bethany looked at the barn when the side door opened. Everett stepped outside and started walking toward the table. He began whistling a familiar melody. She grinned and leaned close to Mandy. "Well, his wait is over."

"Good," Mandy whispered. "I was afraid you had given a thief the keys to your heart."

"One more day in quarantine and I might have." Bethany smiled at Everett as he walked toward them.

A half-grin curved Everett's lips. He glanced back and forth between Bethany and Mandy. "Don't you girls look full of secrets, whispering and grinning in the dark?"

"Never mind that," Mandy said while she removed herself from the splintery tabletop with as much feminine grace as a woman could in a floor-length dress. "Where is my husband?" When Everett pointed at the barn, Mandy brushed the back of her skirt. "What did he do with the louts?"

"He sent them home." Everett spoke to his sister but his eyes were fixed on Bethany. "Are you all right, Beth?" he asked as Mandy tiptoed through the dewy grass and slipped back into the side door of the barn.

"I'm fine." She glanced at the light that spilled from the barn and it momentarily ruined her vision. She focused on Everett as her eyes readjusted to the dark. "Mandy and I were getting some fresh air."

"Yes, the cold air feels good after being stuffed in the barn with two hundred dancing villagers."

Everett loosened his cravat and let it hang unopened around his neck. He lifted his foot to the bench of the picnic table and leaned his forearms upon his knee. "Have you given any thought to my request?"

"Any thought?" She murmured a chuckle. "I have spent the past two weeks thinking of little else."

He leaned an inch closer. "Have you considered me?"

"Yes."

"Him too?"

"Yes, Justin too."

Everett heaved a breath. It puffed into a little cloud then dissipated. He pushed away from the table and took a few steps toward the paddock. One of the horses started walking to the fence. Everett sank his hands into his pockets then walked back and planted his feet close to the table. "I saw him talking to you earlier and—" He clenched his jaw and looked away.

As much as it delighted Bethany to see Everett's willingness to fight for her, once his aggression was stirred it took hours for his pleasant demeanor to return. She preferred him pleasant. Bethany lifted a hand. "Justin has no place in my future."

"Are you sure?" Everett's expression lightened. He boosted himself onto the tabletop and sat beside her where Mandy had been. "Do you feel anything for him?"

Bethany shook her head. "Only concern." When he stared at her with a crease in his brow, she felt the need to expound. "I can tell he is lonely. He doesn't feel welcome here."

"Is that something you sensed or something he said?"

"Both." As Bethany said it she realized it was the only thing Justin had said to her that did coincide with the emotions she sensed from him. "I'm not in love with him, but I do care about him."

"Of course you do, Beth. Your sensitivity makes you compassionate, and that's something I love about you. It's sweet of you to care, but use caution. You should stay away from him." He took her hand and curled her fingers onto his palm. "So you have sorted out your feelings for him, but have you come to a decision about us?"

"I have." She studied his features in the faint light coming from the barn. Her gaze traced the stubble along the line of his jaw to the shadow beneath his lower lip. "I'm sorry to make you wait for my reply. When I came out of quarantine, I was not myself. I had been through a lot. I felt such distance between us and I wasn't prepared for your request. It has taken this long for me to absorb all that you said—especially that part about loving me and waiting these past two years to ask me to court."

He lifted her hand to his lips. "I do love you. And I will wait another two years if you need me to. No matter how it pains me, I will wait. I never want to rush you."

"No, I am ready now—to court, I mean."

A slow smile curved his mouth. "Then I will shower you with love—not to lure you into spending your life with me but as a foretaste of what a life with me would be like. And I will lead us slowly because when we are ready to join our lives, I want you to be able to look back at our courtship without a single regret. Just promise me one thing, Beth."

"What?"

"Promise me you will stay away from Justin Mercer."

# Chapter Ten

Everett drank the last hot sip from his coffee mug while he leaned against the kitchen counter. Roseanna took the empty mug with her sudsy hand. She dunked it in the dishwater and as she wiped it with a wet rag, she glanced at Everett. "Nicholas' sister had her baby. It's a boy." She set the clean mug in the dish rack.

Everett yawned and looked out the kitchen window at the early frost gleaming across the paddock. "I need to get the flock into the shelter today; bad weather is coming."

Roseanna wrung out her rag and laid it over the sink's edge. "The traveler from Woodland brought word about the baby on Saturday, but Nicholas only told me last night during the dance."

Everett nodded as he stepped to the coatrack by the back door. He understood Nicholas' disinclination to share personal information— and appreciated it. As he shrugged into his coat, he felt its pocket for his gloves. The pockets were empty. "Have you seen my work gloves? The brown ones?"

"No, son. Maybe you left them in the barn last night after the dance." Roseanna pulled the plug in the sink and the water gurgled as it swirled down the drain. "You'll probably misplace a lot of things with all that's on your mind: handling the flock, elder meetings, waiting for Bethany's answer..."

"She gave me her answer," Everett mumbled as he searched the pockets of the other coats on the rack. He could not remember where his gloves were because he was still half asleep. Joy over Bethany's acceptance had kept him awake most of the night.

Roseanna tilted her head. "Oh, I'm sorry, son."

"Why? She said yes."

Roseanna clutched both hands to her heart and squealed with delight. "That's wonderful! Well, you should be happy this morning instead of scowling at the frost. She is a sweet one, that Bethany—just like her mother. Oh, I'm happy for you, son! For you and her both."

Everett felt his gloves inside another coat's pocket. He held them up. "Found them. Bye, Mother." As he left the porch, he glanced back at the kitchen window and saw Roseanna's beaming smile. He flashed a grin, then he slid his hands into his gloves and jogged across the frosted grass to the side door of the barn. His flock of over four hundred ewes filled the air with a cacophony of bleats as they waited in the paddock. Everett loved the sound.

He stepped through the barn's side door. Nicholas had already taken down the lanterns, removed the stage, and set up the feeders, and he was shoveling grass hay into the last empty feeder. Though Nicholas had come to the property as a farm hand, he'd quickly proven his worth.

Everett grabbed a pitchfork and started working beside Nicholas. "Sorry I'm late."

"After the amount of work you put into the party last night, I figured you'd sleep until noon." Nicholas' thick sideburns puffed as he grinned. "Besides, you own the place—you don't have to apologize."

"You've already done a full day's work. Thank you."

Nicholas kept spreading hay. "It frosted last night, but I don't trust the clear sky. I think a storm is coming and James agrees. He's got the flock ready to come inside."

"Good. My father would have appreciated you both." Everett scooped the last of the grass hay from the wheelbarrow and propped his pitchfork against the wall. "Is Mercer here yet?"

"Not yet." Nicholas wheeled the empty barrow toward the back of the barn. "He arrives later each day and then complains the whole time he's here."

Everett picked up his pitchfork and followed. "I'll speak to him about his tardiness when he arrives—whenever that might be."

As Nicholas opened the back door, his words were buried in the sound of the bleating sheep. The happiness that arose from Everett's every thought of Bethany was quickly choked by his frustration with Mercer. While Nicholas and James let the sheep inside the building, Everett stood back against the wall. The herding dogs rounded the sheep, forcing them through the barn door. This farm and this flock were his inheritance. He planned to live here in peace and one day make Bethany his wife. So if Mercer wanted to keep his job, he was going to have to change his ways.

* * *

Bethany crouched beside an open-slat shipping crate as she wrapped the last bowl with packing paper. She laid it inside the crate then stood and looked around the pottery yard. All of the orders had been filled, and the tools and supplies had been cleaned and packed into the shed for the winter.

Mrs. Vestal closed the shed doors and secured the latch then lumbered toward Bethany. "The trader said he would be here by noon to pick that up. You can go on home, I'll wait."

Bethany watched Mrs. Vestal grimace and rub her lower back. She hated to see her mentor in pain, but like many of the older folks, Mrs. Vestal refused the gray leaf. Bethany shook her head. "No, I'm happy to wait here. You should go home and rest your back."

"You're a sweet girl, Bethany. And the best apprentice I ever had—you more than worked for your training." Though the air was cold, Mrs. Vestal drew a stained handkerchief from her pocket and dabbed her forehead. "I don't have the pep I used to, and I've got no one to pass the pottery to when the Lord takes me home. You've finished your three years with me. If you want to make a life of it, I'll pass this place on to you one day soon."

The thought of owning the pottery yard thrilled Bethany, but it was unheard of to pass a family inheritance to a nonrelative. She walked close to Mrs. Vestal. "I plan to spend my life as a potter, but don't you want to keep the pottery yard in your family?"

Mrs. Vestal shrugged. "Nicholas loves sheep farming and is working with Everett to get his own flock. And my niece and her husband just had a baby; they have no interest in coming to Good Springs. You're the closest thing I have to a daughter, and you are the best potter we've had in the Land during my lifetime."

Mrs. Vestal's approbation filled Bethany with pride, though she sensed her mentor's sadness. Her eyes blurred with tears as she bent to hug Mrs. Vestal. "Thank you."

Mrs. Vestal's chin quivered as she nodded. "You work here with me until I can't do it anymore, and it's yours. I'll settle the matter with the elders." She cleared her throat and pointed to the shipping crate. "The trader will be here by noon. Latch the gate when you leave."

As Mrs. Vestal left, Bethany stepped into the pottery shelter and leaned against the support post. She looked around the pottery yard again, but this time with a sense of ownership. She expected that completing the three-year apprenticeship would solidify her as a professional potter and make her craftsmanship recognized throughout the Land, but she had not expected to be made the heir of the business. Bethany leaned her head back against the post and grinned up at the clear sky.

"What's got you smiling today, beautiful?"

Bethany flinched and snapped her head toward the familiar voice. "Justin!"

"Sorry. I didn't mean to startle you." Justin stepped under the shelter and slid his thumbs into his belt loops.

She chuckled at herself and moved away from the post. "You didn't. Well, you did, but it's my own fault for daydreaming."

Justin grinned and leaned against the post. "It must've been a good one—you looked happy."

"I am happy." She sighed as she untied the strings of her work apron. "Today was the last day of my apprenticeship."

"Congratulations. So now you're what… master potter?"

"No," Bethany giggled. "Now I'm recognized as a craftsman in the Land and I can work for my own trade."

Justin cast his gaze across the pottery yard and his grin faded. "But trade for what? I don't get it. You all work so hard for nothing."

"What do you mean? We work for our livelihood and we work because every person has something to give. Everyone has a purpose in a community."

She felt his emptiness and his words matched his emotions. She took a step closer to him. "You will have a purpose here. Everett has given you work for now, and I'm sure once you've been here for a while you will find your place in the village. Connor did chores for my father for months before Father realized he would make an excellent schoolteacher. And I wouldn't have learned anything during my last two years of school if it weren't for Connor's instruction. Just give it time—you will find your place."

"You're the only person who seems to think so." Justin pulled his thumbs out of his belt loops. "I just quit the job at Everett's farm."

"Quit? Why?"

"I hated it. The sheep are loud, the whole place stinks, and your boyfriend is a jerk." He held up a hand. "No offense to you—he's just constantly on my case. He acts like I'm an idiot. I was a naval flight officer. Do you know how hard the training is for that position? I have a degree in aerospace engineering. I don't need to get lectured by a sheep farmer about work ethic. The guy is just a twerp."

Though she sensed Justin truly felt mistreated, she disagreed with his assessment of Everett. She wadded her apron into a ball. "I think it was charitable of Everett to give you work. He is a patient, hard-working man. I've known him my whole life and he has always been decent and shown restraint. He is the most kind and humble man I know."

Justin crossed his arms. "It sounds like you're in love with him."

"I am. We are courting." Bethany looked Justin in the eye. "But that's not why I said those things about him—"

"I must admit I'm disappointed," he interrupted.

"In me?"

"No, not in you. You are just doing what's expected of you. I'm disappointed because I feel like I'm losing my only friend here."

Justin's words dejected Bethany. She touched his arm. "No, I'm still your friend."

"Really? Do you think he wants you hanging out with me?" Justin snickered. "Your dad and brother and even Connor have been keeping me away from you. And now that you are dating Everett, they'll probably punish you for even speaking to me."

The grain of truth in Justin's statement made Bethany feel uneasy. The men in her life had made her feel guilty for her desire to befriend Justin. She drew her hand away. "It's not like that. They don't punish me. My father is the overseer of our village and it is important to him that his daughters behave properly. And my brother has always been protective, but there is nothing wrong with that."

"Fine. But why does Connor have authority over you?"

"He was my teacher."

"He's not anymore."

"I don't know." Bethany looked at her fingernails as she thought for a moment. "Connor is a natural leader and he will probably train to be the village overseer one day."

Justin shook his head. "They all control you. All the men in your life control you. Don't you see how the women here act subservient to men?"

"That's not true. Men and women are different, but we know we are equal."

"Not from what I've seen here."

"Take Lydia for example: she was our village's first female physician. No one cared that she took on a position that only men had previously held. She trained and was qualified and devoted to the health of the village. That was all that mattered."

Justin shrugged. "But she still has to answer to a council of male elders. Why aren't there any female elders?"

"I don't know."

"And why not have a female overseer?"

"The position has always been passed down to the overseer's son."

"Then how could Connor one day become overseer? He isn't even from here."

"I don't know. Things are starting to change."

Justin pointed a finger at the chapel across the street. "It's because the men control the women here. They might make you think you have a choice, but you really don't. You don't have a vote on the council or a choice of your profession or a even say in who you can be friends with."

"That's not true. I chose my profession, as did Lydia and Mandy. And any woman here who spends her life making a home and helping her husband has chosen to do so. If a woman demonstrated the leadership qualities it takes to be an elder and had the desire to be on the council, being female would not keep her from it. I wouldn't want that position, nor would any woman I know, but that doesn't make women subservient to men."

"I think this whole society is a patriarchy. You're an adult, but you still obey your father's demands."

"I am under his authority because I live in his home. That's just part of our tradition. I don't like all of the traditions, but I love Everett, and if we marry I will respect his leadership in our home. That doesn't mean I have to answer to every man in the village simply because he is a man. Most men here don't have the qualities my father and the elders have. Father and Connor and Everett deserve my respect, but I can be friends with whomever I choose."

"You really are naïve." Justin blew out a breath and stared into the distance. When he looked back at her, one edge of his mouth curved into a smile. "Besides, a man and a woman who've been attracted to each other don't choose to be friends—they settle for being friends."

Bethany wondered if she should be offended, but only sensed his frustration. She put her hands on her hips and grinned. "Fine, then I choose whom I settle to be friends with." When Justin chuckled at her, she reached her hand to the post that he was leaning against. She picked a flake of old paint from the side of the wooden post and wondered why she no longer sensed the duality in him that had once puzzled her. "You've dropped your pretense with me. I like it, but why now?"

"Like I said—you are my only friend here." Justin pushed away from the post. "I don't like it when my friends are treated badly."

She held up a finger. "Now you are the male who is being protective."

"The difference is: I may disagree with your opinion, but I won't try to take it from you." Justin winked and walked away.

Bethany followed Justin to the gate, but they did not say goodbye. She watched him leave. His head was down while he crossed the cobblestone street. She felt sorry for him. His figure decreased from her perspective as he passed the chapel and trudged up the incline beside the graveyard toward his borrowed cabin. He was right in that he had no place in the community. She felt his loneliness and was saddened that he had no family or purpose in the Land, but she was determined to be his friend.

* * *

After Everett moved the flock into the barn, he left Nicholas to feed the other animals and marched down the road toward the Colburn property. His admonition to Mercer had led to a hostile argument and ended in Mercer quitting the job. He was glad to have Mercer off his farm, but he could not get him out of his mind.

As Everett left the gravel road and cut across the yard to the Colburns' barn, he increased his pace in anticipation of the pleasurable release of sparring. The brutal form of athleticism Connor had brought to the Land— and secretly taught Levi and Everett—proved to be a valuable skill when they once fought to protect their village. But that was over a year ago, and with a baby for Connor and marriage for Levi, the men had fallen out of practice. Everett longed to return to the sport—both for its physical release and to stay prepared should he ever need to use the art again.

The barn door was ajar, so Everett slipped inside and pulled it shut. Levi was leaning against a stall gate, winding a spool of the copper wire that Connor had salvaged from space debris long ago. Connor was inside the stall bent over a green metal box. Everett flipped his hair off his forehead as he walked toward Levi. "Mandy said you would be here."

Levi wound the last length of wire. "What's wrong?"

"It has been too long since we've sparred, that's what's wrong."

Connor popped a knob off the top of the radio transmitter and began to wipe it with a rag. "You have only been dating Bethany one day and she's got you ready to throw, huh?"

Levi chuckled. "You better get used to it—she's not going to want to get married for a long time."

Connor laughed, too, but Everett did not. He shook his head. "It has nothing to do with her. The thought of her is the only thing that's kept me calm today. I wanted to snap his head off."

"Who? Mercer?" Connor asked as he pushed the knob back into place on the radio.

"Of course Mercer."

Connor nodded and dropped his rag atop the transmitter then walked out of the stall and toward the front of the barn. As he moved a cart out of the open area and pushed it to the back of the barn, Levi opened a wooden trunk and pulled out two pairs of leather sparring gloves. Everett took off his coat and began rolling up his sleeves. He turned back to the hay-strewn open space of the shadowy barn and looked at the two men he trusted most. They were ready to fight. Everett grinned and stretched his neck to either side. "Just like old times."

Connor raised a palm. "Everett, you seem really ticked. Are you sure you want to spar right now? If you lose focus, you're going to get hurt."

Levi tossed one pair of gloves to Everett and the other to Connor. "Less talk, more action."

Everett pulled on the homemade sparring gloves he used to wear weekly when Connor first trained him to fight. His pulse increased as he stepped forward and they tapped gloves.

* * *

After the trader picked up the shipment, Bethany walked out of the pottery yard for the last time as an apprentice. She carefully secured the latch but held onto the gate as she remembered when she first visited the pottery yard with her class. During Mrs. Vestal's demonstration, Bethany's interest had grown with every movement of the clay. By the end of the visit, she surprised Mrs. Vestal with an exuberant request to apprentice. When Bethany told her father, he gave a lecture on responsibility and—though skeptical of her dedication to three years of work, which overlapped with her required schooling—he permitted it. That was three years ago. Now her apprenticeship was complete.

She let go of the gate and walked away from the pottery yard, alone and cold on a clear afternoon. There was neither a ceremony for her efforts like Lydia received when she became a doctor, nor a great struggle for independence like Levi went through when he shirked tradition and chose a profession that differed from his father's. Bethany simply latched a gate and walked away, her only congratulations thus far from a man she had been told to avoid.

As Bethany passed the path that led through a swath of forest to the beach, she raised her collar to shield her neck from the cold wind. She glanced back at the path and thought of when she first met Justin. He had staggered down that path and into her life. Now she and Everett were courting and Justin was lonely and purposeless in the Land. Bethany heard her father's voice calling her name. She looked back at the path as John jogged out of the forest. His wind-torn hair and wide eyes made him look frightened, though Bethany doubted anything could startle her father.

She walked back to the path and smiled at him. "Don't you look worrisome?"

"Bethany, get Connor. Quickly!" John panted between words. "There is a ship on the horizon. Go find Connor!"

"What do you mean?"

"There was no school today, so he is probably at home. Tell him to get the telescope and meet me at the cairn on the shore. Then go get Justin Mercer and tell him to meet us there too."

"Is it Mercer's ship?"

"I am not sure." John pointed toward home. "Go now!"

While her father disappeared back into the forest toward the shore, Bethany lifted the front of her skirt and ran to the house. She was out of breath and her legs burned as she opened the back door and hurried into the kitchen. Lydia was standing near the sink, rinsing a freshly plucked chicken.

"Where's Connor?" Bethany huffed.

"In the barn, last I knew. What's wrong?"

Bethany ran out of the kitchen without closing the door or answering Lydia. Her skirt swished as she hurried through the grass. She reached the barn and threw the door open. Levi was standing inside with his back to the door. As she stepped into the darkened barn she saw Connor punch Everett in the face. She gasped as Everett's head snapped back. Blood spurted from his nose and he fell to the ground. Levi moved quickly into Bethany's line of sight. He grabbed her by the arms and pushed her outside. Before she could see anything else, Levi kicked the door closed behind him.

"What are you doing here?" he demanded.

"Father sent me. What is Connor doing? Is Everett all right?"

As she reached for the barn door, Levi blocked her hand. "You're not allowed in there when we're sparring."

"Sparring? I didn't know. Father sent me to get Connor. Is Everett hurt?"

"He's okay, Beth." Connor's muffled voice came from inside the barn.

Levi's expression softened and he nodded. "He'll be fine. What does Father need?"

Bethany drew a breath and tried to clear her mind of the image of Everett getting hit. She recalled her father's panicked words. "He said there is a ship on the horizon. He wants Connor to get the—"

"A ship?" Levi interrupted.

"Yes, a ship. He wants Connor to get the telescope and meet him on the shore."

The barn door popped open a few inches and Connor slid out. "Where on the shore does he want me to meet him?"

"At the cairn," she answered.

Connor and Levi exchanged a look. Connor threw a pair of bulky leather gloves on the ground and marched toward the house. Levi kept a loose grip on Bethany's arm and urged her forward as they followed Connor. She pulled her arm away from her brother. "Father told me to go get Justin too."

Connor glanced over his shoulder at her. "No! Levi can get Mercer. You need to go in the house and stay there."

Irritated by the plethora of men telling her what to do, Bethany stopped walking. Levi looked behind her and nodded once at someone, then he diverged from the path and jogged toward the road to go get Justin.

Everett came from behind her. "Come on, Beth. I'll go inside with you."

"I don't need a chaperone," she protested, though Everett was the one man she would listen to. She clamped her arms around her body and did not look at Everett as they followed Connor to the house. He had been hurt and he would not want her to look.

As they stepped into the kitchen, Lydia glanced up from the chicken she was preparing. "Would someone please tell me what is going on? Good heavens, Everett! What happened to your face?"

Connor moved quickly through the kitchen toward the parlor. "Your dad is at the shore. He wants me to meet him with the telescope. He says there is a ship on the horizon."

"A ship?" Lydia dropped the chicken into the pan with a fleshy splat. "Connor?"

"Yes, a ship," he said coolly as he came back into the kitchen carrying an old telescope. He kissed the top of Lydia's head. "I'm sure it's nothing, but we're going to go look. Bethany is to stay here with you."

"All right." Lydia turned to Everett, who was bent over the sink washing his face. "So what happened to you?"

"We were sparring." Connor answered for Everett as he walked past the sink to the door.

"I forgot how fast Connor moves," Everett mumbled as he filled his cupped hands with water.

"I told you not to spar while you're angry." Connor patted Everett's bent back then walked out the door. "Meet us at the shore when you're done, Everett."

Bethany stood between the sink and the table, lost in the flurry of glances and questions. She was half stunned and half offended. Her legs burned from running, and her arm ached where Levi had grabbed her to get her out of the barn. He had tried to protect her from seeing their brutal hobby, and she had only done what she'd been told to do. Still, she felt guilty.

Lydia glanced at her. "Do you want to help me with dinner?"

Bethany did not answer. The image of Everett getting hit was burned into her mind. She watched him wash his face and felt both horrified and thrilled by what she had witnessed. She stepped to the cupboard and drew out a tea towel. When Everett moved his foot off the sink pedal, the water stopped flowing from the faucet. As she handed him the towel, he looked her in the eye. He dried his face and winced when he wiped his red cheek.

Lydia wedged between them and washed her hands. "Let me have a look."

Everett stepped back. "No, Lydia, it's nothing."

"It's Doctor Bradshaw to you, and I'll determine if it's nothing," she said as she reached a hand up to his face.

Bethany turned away and picked at her cuticles. Lydia mumbled something, and Everett sucked in a breath. Bethany leaned her back against the kitchen counter and stared at the polished wooden beam above the doorway that led into the parlor.

"You didn't break any bones," Lydia said to Everett. "Do you want me to put some gray leaf salve on the cut?"

"No, I'm fine. Really."

"Lydia?" Isabella's gravelly voice called from the back bedroom.

"I'll go," Bethany said.

"No, Bethany. I'll take care of her." As Lydia walked toward Isabella's room, she pointed at the chicken. "Put that in the oven for me, please."

Bethany moved to the oven and reached for a potholder to turn the handle. She sensed Everett was watching her as she picked up the pan and slid it into the hot oven. The iron stove clanged as she closed the oven door. She dropped the potholder onto the countertop. "Are you all right?"

"Yes." Everett turned his face away. "Are you?"

"No."

"I'm sorry you saw that."

"I'm not."

Everett snorted. "Great, well, I'm going to go crawl in a hole and die now."

Dark pieces of damp hair were stuck to his forehead. His red swollen cheek made the green of his eyes look fierce. "After years of wondering what men look like while they are fighting, I finally know."

"I'm glad you got something out of it," he said sarcastically. "I don't want you to see me get hurt."

She understood humiliation—it was what she had felt moments before when several men were telling her what to do and where to look and where not to look all at the same time. Considering her conversation with Justin, she should probably be angry with them—maybe her life was controlled by men. But then she looked at Everett and his cut cheek and the drips of blood on his cuffed sleeve. He was the man she loved and he was trying to protect her. He did not want to control her any more than she wanted to control him. She stepped closer to him. "Do you enjoy sparring?"

"I love it."

"Then it is part of you and I will have to get used to you getting hurt once in a while." She reached her hand to his arm. "But if you try to hide your hurt from me, you're only robbing me of the chance to love you through it."

Everett covered her hand with his. "Your father told me your mother used to say that to him."

"Really?" Bethany wondered why she never knew. Everett glanced out the window. He wanted to get to the shore. She wanted to go too. "Let me come with you."

"No, Beth. You have to stay here."

"Please. If there is a ship, I want to see it."

"It's not safe." Everett patted her hand then stepped to the door. "You're not coming. I love you, but you're not coming."

# Chapter Eleven

As he trekked the sandy path to the cairn on the shore, Everett focused on the dark blemish that scarred the horizon. Connor was pointing a telescope at the object on the sea. John was leaning against a tall stack of stones that marked the place where the founders first came ashore in eighteen sixty-one. Both men glanced back at Everett as he stepped behind them.

The blur on the ocean appeared too flat and inelegant to be a ship, but its menacing bulk made Everett nervous. His toes curled inside his boots. "It doesn't look like a ship."

John's graying hair blew across his forehead as he turned to Everett. "That is what I first thought. It certainly does not resemble any of the illustrations in our founders' writings, but Connor says it is most definitely a ship."

"Is it Mercer's?" Everett asked Connor.

"No, it's not. I have no idea where the icebreaker is. He drifted here on a dinghy in the middle of the night when he came to the Land. His ship could be miles from here." Connor pulled his face away from the telescope and rubbed one eye with the back of his hand. Then he pointed at the ship on the ocean. "That is an aircraft carrier."

"Is it American?"

"It's definitely a Unified States platform, but I can't tell how close it is to the coast."

Everett looked out at the blurry ship. "It looks like it's on the horizon. On a clear day on land, that would be about three miles away. Why can't you tell how far away it is?"

Connor stepped back from the telescope. "The visual is skewed looking out to sea from here because of the atmosphere around the Land. That ship could be one mile from us, it could be ten." He pointed to the telescope. "Have a look."

Everett moved to the telescope and bent to look through the brass eyepiece. He squeezed the other eye shut as he focused on the hazy V-shape that rose out of the sea. The ship's flat upper portion spread wide over the water, and dark lines blurred above the deck on one side. "What's that sticking up on the left?"

"That's called the island. It houses flight deck control, the navigation bridge, the chartroom— or did you mean the mast on top of the island?"

"I don't know what I'm looking at." Everett stepped back and John took a turn at the telescope. Everett glanced at Connor. "Do you think the people on that ship can see us?"

"No, I don't. If it were possible to see the Land from out there, the crew would have a perfect visual of us. Believe me, they have better technology than an antique mariner's telescope. And if they could detect the Land, they would have already determined the resources here and the lack of defense. This place would be buzzing with activity that we don't want. They have no idea this land is—"

Connor stopped talking and looked back at the path.

Everett followed Connor's line of sight. Levi and Mercer were approaching the shore. "Great," Everett mumbled when he saw Mercer. John pulled his eye away from the telescope and sent Everett a parental look.

Levi was scowling at the ship as he walked toward the cairn, but Mercer's face was stretched with the stupidest looking smile Everett had ever seen. Levi stopped beside Everett while Mercer walked straight to the telescope and looked at the ship.

"Oh yeah! Look at that beauty!" Mercer sang out like an excited schoolgirl. "I've never been so happy to see a platform in my life. Ford class, I'd say. What do you think, Bradshaw?"

"Probably," Connor replied.

"The flight deck's empty."

"I noticed." Connor sounded concerned. "Completely empty."

"Has it moved?"

"No, I think it's anchored."

Mercer twisted the brass rings as if the telescope needed adjusting. Then he stuck his face to the eyepiece again. "You were right: there's something wrong with the atmosphere around here. It's still a beautiful sight. Hooyah!"

Everett and Levi glanced at each other. Levi shrugged. Mercer prattled on about how wonderful it was to see the ship. John stepped toward Mercer and put a hand on his back. Everett thought that was more friendliness than Mercer deserved, and looked away. As far as he was concerned Mercer had brought them infection, insolence, and now possible invasion.

"Justin," John said to Mercer, "do you believe the crew on that ship can see the Land?"

"No. They would be all over this place if they knew it was here." Then Mercer looked at Connor. "Let's fire off a few flares. The dinghy is still in your shed, right? It's got a kit—"

John raised a palm. "Please do not send any signals."

"Don't worry, John. We won't." Connor's first use of an authoritative tone over Mercer pleased Everett. Connor looked at Mercer. "We don't want the Land to be detected."

Mercer stepped back and furrowed his brow. "You've got to be kidding me! Can you honestly say that if there is a chance for you to get on that platform, you won't take it?"

"Absolutely not. I have a family here."

"A lot of people on that ship have a family somewhere, Bradshaw. Kiss your wife and baby goodbye like a good sailor and get back on that ship."

"Sailor?" Levi chuckled. "I thought you were a pilot."

"I thought you both were pilots," John's gaze shifted between Connor and Mercer.

Connor shook his head. "I'm a naval aviator— was a naval aviator. Mercer was a naval flight officer."

John scratched his beard. "What is the difference?"

"I can land aircraft on a platform for starters," Connor smirked.

Mercer threw up his hands. "Hey, I can land aircraft too."

"Yeah, on a ten thousand foot immobile runway—not on a platform and forget a pitching deck." Connor seemed to be enjoying his banter with Mercer, but it made Everett wonder if Connor would remain loyal to the Land.

"So what?" Mercer laughed. "You couldn't do it anymore. Those are perishable skills."

Connor glanced at John, Levi, and Everett, then his grin disappeared and he crossed his arms. He looked back at Mercer. "You may be eager to get your old life back, but this is my life now. I'm dead to the outside world. I worked through that three years ago. I have to protect my family and my village. Besides, I've seen what the currents around the Land can do, and it may not be possible to make it out to that ship."

* * *

Everett paced the wooden planks of the chapel's entryway while the village elders gathered in the front pews. He stopped at one of the doors and peered out its sliver of a window. Though late afternoon, the autumn daylight was already waning. A few villagers milled around outside the chapel, curious as to the cause of the emergency elder meeting. Everett scanned the cobblestone street. Connor and Mercer were nowhere in sight. Surely Connor could still be trusted. Surely he would not let Mercer turn on the radio transmitter and contact the ship.

John's gentle baritone reverberated through the cavernous sanctuary as he stood at the front of the chapel. He was explaining the ship on the horizon, Connor's belief that the ship's crew could not see the Land, and Mercer's desire to try to row out to the ship. Though the elders knew about Mercer's situation, their comments reflected their surprise with his dissatisfaction of life in the Land.

Everett turned away from the window and walked along the outside aisle to the front pews where the elders were discussing the situation. As soon as he sat beside Levi in the pew behind the elders, Connor and Mercer walked in the chapel. Silence shrouded the meeting as the elders turned and watched the two former warriors strut down the center aisle of the village church.

John motioned to the front pew. "Have a seat up here please, gentlemen."

As Connor sat on the front row, he looked back at Levi and Everett and gave one short nod. Levi returned the nod. Though Everett knew it was Connor's way of reassuring them, he did not return the gesture. Connor creased his brow as he looked at Everett for a moment, then he turned his attention to John.

John laid his pencil on the podium and stepped to the front pew. "Justin, the elders are unclear on why you would risk your life to leave the Land."

Mercer rested his arm along the back of the pew and glanced at the other men. "I don't belong here."

John gave Mercer a moment to elaborate, but Mercer remained silent.

Connor shifted sideways. "After we monitored the ship this afternoon, Mercer and I discussed at length what we believe is happening out there. After years of war, the outside world is plagued with a tuberculosis epidemic and there isn't enough medicine. We noticed an unusual lack of aircraft and activity on the ship's flight deck. We wonder if anyone is still alive on that ship, and if they are—due to Mercer's experience trying to locate the Land—we doubt they know the Land is here. Mercer wants to return to the outside world and is certain he should attempt to reach the carrier."

Everett watched Connor speak for Mercer. The distrust he felt toward Connor churned his stomach. After all he had been through with Connor, Everett wanted to trust him, but he could not shake the feeling that Mercer was influencing Connor away from them. Everett could not hold his tongue another moment. "And what about you, Connor? Do you want to leave also?"

Connor looked back at Everett, as did several elders. His dark eyes held an intensity that reflected the sting of Everett's doubt. "No. I am certain my place is here in the Land." He held Everett's gaze even as John began speaking again. Finally, Everett looked away.

"Thank you, Connor," John said. Then he turned to Mercer. "What is your plan?"

"If the carrier is still there in the morning, I want to row out. The outboard motor on the dinghy still has fuel in it. My friend got communications back up as I was leaving our ship. He was going to send a message to the navy to come and help me. Even though he is probably dead by now, he did that for me, so if the carrier is here because it received that message, I owe it to him to—" Mercer's voice broke. He pulled his arm off the pew and cleared his throat. "After I saw Connor drift toward this land, I spent three years trying to get back here. I didn't have a chance to go to America after the crash—they reassigned me to Antarctica. Then communications went down and I didn't think I'd ever make it home, so I just focused on finding this land. You people have a good thing going here. I feel like I've gone back in time. But if there is a chance to return to my country, I want to do it. The day my friend got the communications back up I was crazy with fever and left the ship. Now there is an American carrier within reach and I have to try to make it out there. I don't belong here; I belong out there."

John nodded. "Thank you, Justin. I appreciate your honesty. I know this has been frustrating for you." He looked around at the elders. "I will assent to Justin's request to leave. Does anyone object?"

Mr. McIntosh, seated on the second row, lifted his hand. "It sounds like he will be rowing to his death, like Frank Roberts and the boys did a few years ago. Does he have any idea about the deadly currents surrounding our shore?"

Mercer straightened his spine. "I'm fully trained for water survival. I know how to respect the sea."

"Your chances of making it to that ship are low," Mr. McIntosh said, speaking directly to Mercer.

"I understand. My chances of making it here were also low, but I made it."

Mr. McIntosh shrugged.

John nodded. "Anyone else?"

"I don't object," Mark Cotter spoke up from the pew in front of Everett, "but how will we know if he makes it to the ship?"

"Good question," Everett muttered.

Connor answered, "We do not believe anyone on the ship can see or detect the Land. If

Mercer makes it to the ship, he will not mention the Land to anyone. We may never know if he makes it to the ship, but we will know that we have not been detected if the ship leaves."

Mr. McIntosh wiped his brow. "Then I am eager for that ship leave the horizon."

"Me too," Everett mumbled. Levi heard him and nodded.

When other men began to chime their agreement, John spread his hands. "Are there any objections to Justin leaving the Land?" When no one spoke, John continued. "Very well. Justin, Connor will help you get your boat ready for the morning. If there is anything you need, please let us know."

"Actually, I would like to take some gray leaf medicine with me."

"Of course," John quickly agreed.

"And some seeds." Mercer added.

John's brow furrowed. "Seeds?"

"So I can plant gray leaf trees in America—if I make it home."

Levi glanced at Everett. Everett shook his head. He looked at the other elders. No one objected, so Everett stood. "If seeds of the gray leaf tree are taken to the outside world and they know what it can do, they will be too impatient for the trees to mature. They will focus on finding the source. When he tells them the Land is full of gray leaf trees, his idea is likely to get us invaded."

Connor lifted a hand. "It was my idea. The gray leaf tree cured his disease and saved Bethany. It may be the only thing that can bring healing to the nations."

Everett looked to John, hoping the overseer would intervene. When he said nothing, Everett sat back down, defeated.

Connor glanced back at Everett. "Mercer has promised never to mention the Land to anyone."

Levi raised a finger. "What if they ask where he got the seeds?"

"I'll say they were floating on the ocean. I have no problem with lying if I need to." Mercer grinned with a confidence that made Everett want to leap over two rows of elders and pound the smirk off his lying face.

Everett glowered at Mercer. "Then how do we know you aren't lying now?"

John lifted his chin. "Thank you, Everett, that is enough. If Justin makes it to the ship, I trust he will not speak of the Land. If the Land has already been detected, I trust Justin to be our liaison and provide diplomacy. If Justin cannot make it to the ship and returns to Good Springs, we will help him find his place in the village. Justin, you may leave at sunrise. Lydia will give you whatever medicine you need, and we trust that you will keep your word. We will pray for your safe return to your homeland and we will watch for the ship to move away from our shore. Meeting adjourned."

Everett rubbed his sweaty palms on his pants and glanced up as the elders stood from their seats and walked to the chapel doors. John put a hand on Mercer's back and said something to him. Connor followed the elders, then he stopped when he approached the pew where Levi and Everett sat. Levi stood, but Everett waited a moment before he joined them. Connor's gaze was fixed on the men leaving the chapel, but he angled his head toward Everett and Levi. "I need to run an idea past you guys before I mention it to John."

"What is it?" Levi asked.

"The radio transmitter in the barn," Connor whispered, "I want to send it with Mercer in the morning. As he rows out he could use it to tell us if he makes it to the ship and if the Land is visible from out there."

Everett shook his head. "The aircraft carrier could pick up his transmission."

"But it wouldn't matter because we wouldn't be sending any signals from the Land. He could keep his comments vague and call for their help in between so it wouldn't sound like he was relaying information to anyone."

"I don't know," Levi said as he crossed his arms. "Can we trust him with a radio transmitter? What if he sends a signal before he leaves?"

"He doesn't know we have the radio and I won't tell him until he's about to leave tomorrow morning." Connor glanced from Levi to Everett.

There was no reason to doubt Connor's sincerity, but the potential to further jeopardize the Land's safety seemed to be escalating. Everett flipped his hair off his forehead and glanced at Mercer and John, who were standing near the chapel door. "I don't trust him."

"None of us do," Connor agreed. "But it would be helpful to know if the Land is visible from the sea or if there really is something protecting it. I've wanted this confirmation for three years. This may be our chance to find out—to finally live in peace knowing we are safe or confirmation that we need to make weapons and send a team of explorers to the mountain range to stake out hiding places. This may be our only chance to find out if the Land is truly in danger of invasion, and I say we take it."

* * *

Bethany stood near the table, laying out five place settings while Lydia helped Isabella to the kitchen. The back door opened and a blast of cold air swirled into the room as John and Connor entered. The men ended a private conversation in hushed tones, piquing Bethany's curiosity.

Connor greeted Lydia with a kiss, then he whispered something to her and she blushed. He pulled his chair out from the table to sit, but she pointed at the sink and he stepped away from the table and washed his hands. John squeezed Bethany's shoulder as he passed her. "Quite a day, was it not? Go ahead and eat—I will be back in few minutes."

As John disappeared up the stairs, Bethany filled Isabella's plate then sat at the side of the table by the hearth. Connor said the blessing and reached for the serving spoon that was tucked into the edge of Lydia's steaming chicken casserole. Lydia sat beside him and gave him a half smile as she snapped her napkin open and laid it on her lap.

John shuffled back into the kitchen and heaved a sigh as he sat at the head of the table. "Pass the bread, please, Bethany."

Bethany glanced at her father as she set the breadbasket in his waiting hand. "Did the elders come to a decision?"

"We did." John took a roll and set the basket near Connor. "Justin will leave at sunrise."

Even though she knew it was coming, the news shocked Bethany. Her breath caught and she dropped her fork on her plate. The unmannerly clink drew everyone's attention. Isabella flinched, Lydia scowled, Connor raised his eyebrows, and John's chewing jaw went still. Bethany pushed back from the table. "No,

Father! He will die. He will drown and you know it. Remember what happened to Luke and Walter? Lydia, you've experienced the ocean's violence. Has everyone forgotten that? Don't let him go, Father. Please. He will die."

"Beth," Connor said her name like she was a child. He patted the air as if to calm her from across the table. "He needs to try to reach that ship."

"No, he doesn't. He will die out there. Or is that what you want?" She glanced back and forth between her father and Connor as she sent out the accusation, hoping one of them would feel convicted. "Justin was right: I am his only friend here. I cannot believe neither of you care about a man's life. He will drown in the ocean just like Luke and Walter did."

Lydia left the table and busied herself at the sink. Connor set down his fork. "Neither Luke nor Walter knew how to swim. Mercer has undergone extensive water survival training in the navy. I am not worried about him drowning. He will be smart about it and will return before dark if he can't reach the ship. And as far as you being his only friend: he is not your friend, Bethany."

"Connor is right," John interjected. "His intentions with you have not been honorable."

Bethany detested the feeling of everyone being against her and guessed that was how Justin had felt the whole time he'd been in the Land. She shook her head. "He shouldn't be sent away just because he doesn't share our customs. He hasn't had a fair chance here. Especially from you," she said as she looked at Connor. "He is your countryman and fought beside you in war. You should try to help him, not make him leave."

Connor leaned an elbow on the table and pointed at her. "You and Everett make quite a pair. He's mad right now because he thinks I've taken Mercer's side and that I'm going to leave the Land too, and you're mad because you don't think I've stood up for Mercer. You are both wrong. Do you want to know what I've been doing? I've been spending every evening with Mercer trying to keep him from ruining you, from upsetting the village, and from exposing the Land. He knows the elders here won't enforce their authority over him, so I've had to work hard to keep him cooperating. If he wants to leave, I'm going to help him go. He has the training and the ability to get to that ship—if it is even possible—and he is willing to keep his mouth shut about this place, but if anybody riles him any more, he's liable to renege on that promise. So stay away from him, and Everett had better hold his peace for one more night, too."

Connor leaned back in his chair. Bethany stared at her hands, but she could feel Connor still looking at her. She felt bad for upsetting him, but she also felt bad for Justin. Her chin began to quiver and she tried to make it stop. "Can I at least tell him goodbye?"

"No," John answered. "Connor and I are going to help him get his boat to the water tomorrow at sunrise. I will tell him for you."

# Chapter Twelve

Bethany stacked clean dinner plates into the cupboard. The clank of their ceramic edges echoed through the quiet kitchen. She folded a damp dishtowel and wiped the empty table, then glanced at Andrew. He was sleeping in his bassinet, and the only movement of his tiny body came from the gentle rise and fall of his respiration. She watched the baby for a moment, and then blew out a heavy breath under the weight of her worry for Justin. If he knew someone cared, he may not make such a dangerous choice like going into the ocean. And if it were not for such strict cultural boundaries, she could go to him and tell him she cared.

Bethany flinched when someone tapped on the window of the back door. She turned to see Roseanna Foster, who was wrapped in a black woolen shawl. Roseanna opened the back door and let herself in. "Hello, Bethany." She flashed a friendly smile as she glanced around the room. "Where is everyone?"

Bethany wiped the table once more. "Aunt Isabella went to bed and Lydia is in the cottage with a patient. Father and Connor are helping Justin get his boat ready for tomorrow."

"Good. I was hoping I could speak with you in private." Roseanna unfurled her shawl and draped it over the coat hooks on the wall behind the door. "When Everett got home, he told me what happened today."

"Which part?" She asked as she pulled a chair away from the table and motioned for Roseanna to sit.

"About the ship and about Justin leaving tomorrow."

"Did Everett send you to speak to me?"

Roseanna frowned at the question as she lowered herself into the seat. "No. He is at Levi's and doesn't even know I'm here. When he told me Justin would be rowing out to sea in the morning, my first thought was of you. I know the men aren't friendly with Justin, especially my son, but you spent ten days in quarantine with him and you form attachments easily. I wanted to see how you were taking it."

"Thank you, Mrs. Foster—"

"You're grown now—call me Roseanna."

"Oh, thank you, Roseanna..." Bethany sat and laid the dishtowel on the table. "I'm in love with Everett and—"

"I'm glad to hear it!" Roseanna interrupted, beaming.

"Yes, well. He detests Justin. My father and brother and brother-in-law all detest Justin. They all tell me to stay away from him, but..."

"But?"

"But I'm his only friend. I can feel his loneliness and my heart hurts for him. I don't think he has been given a fair chance. Connor said Justin wants to leave and the elders aren't making him go. Justin told me himself he doesn't feel like he belongs here. But I watched two of my friends die in the ocean once, and I don't want that to happen to Justin." Tears warmed the corners of Bethany's eyes. She folded the edge of the dishtowel. "He may die tomorrow and they won't let me say goodbye to him."

Roseanna inclined her head as she patted Bethany's arm. "I had a feeling this would be tearing you up inside. You are sensitive—you inherited that from your mother. Sweet Bethany. A girl should have her mother on days like these. I'm sorry I didn't see it sooner."

Bethany blotted her tears with the towel and looked at Roseanna. "Thank you."

"I don't know what for."

"You came. You knew I was hurting and you came. That's what I want to do for Justin, but I can't, can I?"

Roseanna shook her head. "No, love. You should respect your father and Connor and Everett and do as they say. They are trying to protect you and you must let them. That's one of the ways men like them show love—by being protective. It's not just men, I suppose. I must admit when I think of a man I don't know trying to get you alone, something rises up inside of me that makes me want to protect you, too. Lydia is the same way. You're a sweet girl, and young, so we all want to keep you safe. I understand it's hard on you, but you should stay away from Justin."

"Stay away from Justin," Bethany repeated the words she had been told so many times. She nodded her head and drew a deep breath. "Thank you, Roseanna."

\* \* \*

The quilt rustled as Bethany rolled onto her side. Bluish light from the full moon shone through the space between the frilly curtains on her window. She pushed the covers away and sat on the edge of the mattress. As she stared at the oval moon, she wondered if Justin were still awake too. Of course he would be—he was the one who was going to die in a few hours.

She took slow, quiet steps to her dressing table and sat on its cushioned seat in front of the mirror. The hours of tossing and turning in bed had tangled her hair. She watched her moonlit reflection as she tugged the comb through the knots and thought of Justin. He may not belong in the Land, he may not like her village or her family and friends, and he may not share their customs or sense of propriety, but he was still human and deserved the kindness of a friend. She picked up her silver bracelet and fastened its clasp beneath her wrist. As she touched the little charm that dangled from the bracelet, she remembered what it was like being locked in quarantine, alone and bored. It was Justin who talked to her and entertained her. Now he was stuck in the Land, alone and bored. She owed it to him to at least say goodbye and let him know there was one person who saw him as a human being. More than that, she needed to know he was leaving on his own accord and that he was truly aware of the ocean's danger.

Bethany tiptoed to her open wardrobe and pulled a red velvet dress off its hanger. After lacing her leather ankle boots, she picked up her woolen coat and draped it over her arm, then she slowly opened her bedroom door, turning its knob in small increments to keep it from squeaking. She held her breath as she closed it, hoping no one would notice she was gone. Then she crept down the stairs, through the kitchen, and out the back door.

As Bethany buried her arms into the sleeves of her thick coat, she glanced up at the clear night sky. The full oval moon—now directly overhead—lit her path as she furtively hurried away from her family's safe, warm home and into the village. There was not a soul in sight and she found it both terrifying and comforting to know she would not be seen going to a man's house alone. Justin had been right: Bethany was not like the rest of them. She understood what he was going through. Knowing that she was doing the right thing impelled her past the shadowy graveyard to the old cabin where Justin was spending his last night in the Land.

The cabin's porch steps creaked as she climbed them. Warm light from a fire inside colored the thin muslin curtains over the front window. She hoped he was still awake as she knocked on the dense wood door. A cold breeze whipped through the porch and brought a copper wind chime to life. Bethany flinched as the flat tones sang through the air. She knocked again—this time louder—and heard footsteps on the other side of the door.

Justin opened the door, shirtless. He stared at her and then a slight grin curved his lips. "Hey, beautiful."

"I'm so sorry to bother you this late at night." Bethany glanced at the dark lines of the tattoo on his chest, then up at his half-closed eyes. "May I come in?"

He stepped back and held the door open. The warmth of the fire felt good on Bethany's cold face. She unbuttoned her coat as she walked into the cabin's only room. When she turned back to Justin, she noticed he had locked the door and she remembered how dangerous

Connor said it was to live in the outside world. She wished there were a way Justin could stay in the Land where it was safe.

"Have a seat," Justin motioned to the short divan pushed against the timber wall. He picked up a silver flask as he passed the table then held it up. "Would you like a drink?"

"No, thank you." Bethany shrugged out of her coat and flopped it over the arm of the divan as she sat. Though he had only lived in the cabin a month, it smelled like him: mysterious and masculine. She watched him step to the divan and thought his gait looked a bit staggered, but it was the middle of the night. "Did I wake you?"

"No."

"I couldn't sleep either. I had to make sure you were all right." She watched his face, hoping to see a sign of approval for her kind gesture.

"I'm fine." He pressed the bottle against his lips and took a swig, then grimaced as he swallowed. "But that's not why you came."

"I know you aren't happy here and I hate that no one seems to be giving you a fair chance, but you don't have to leave."

"Yes, I do."

"Are they making you go?"

"No, it was my decision. But they are making it easy." He sat beside her and exhaled audibly. The pungent scent on his breath stung her nose and she glanced at the flask. He set it on the doily-topped table beside the divan and put his arm across the cushion behind her. "I was hoping you would come see me tonight."

"Really?" She saw the light hit his eyes and recognized his look of desire. She scooted back an inch, but she was already pressed into the corner of the short seat. "Like I said: I came to make sure you were all right."

He chortled and moved his hand to her thigh. "I know the real reason you're here. You've wanted me since the minute we met."

"Justin!" She scolded as she pushed his hand off her leg. "I came here to warn you about the ocean. You have no idea how dangerous the currents are around the Land and I've seen—"

"You came to warn me?"

"Yes, because—"

"I don't buy it." His voice was quiet as he moved in close. "I'll be fine, babe. I know what I'm doing. And so do you."

Bethany tried to sense his emotions, wanting to detect something positive in his intentions but she only felt his arrogance and anger. She drew her head back. "I thought we were friends." He shook his head and reached for his flask. As he took another drink, she looked at the bottle. "Is that something you brought with you to the Land?"

"It's whiskey. I found it in the emergency supplies when Connor and I were getting the boat ready tonight. Felt like I struck gold when I saw it. Want a sip? It'll loosen you up a bit."

"No, thank you." Her venture outside the cultural boundaries was not being received as well meaning but as a solicitation beyond her intentions. She stood and reached for her coat. "I should leave."

"Don't go." He sank his hands into her hips and spun her around. "This is what you really came here for—" He pressed his mouth against hers. She tasted the drink on his lips and shoved her arms against his bare chest. His fingers moved and tightened around her waist. She feared he was not going to let go. Her heart hammered in her throat; everyone had been right about him. They had all tried to warn her: Connor and her father and Lydia and Everett and—

Justin released her and drew a breath. She gripped her coat and backed away from him. For every step she took closer to the door he took one toward her. Then his expression changed. He stopped walking and wiped both hands across his face. "What am I doing? I am so sorry. I'm being such a jerk. Listen please, I'm sorry. I don't know what came over me."

His sudden vicissitude held genuine remorse, but she no longer pitied him. "Justin, how could you?"

"I can't help it. You're so young and you show up at my place in the middle of the night and what am I supposed to think? Don't leave. Please, forgive me, beautiful."

"Don't call me that."

"Look, don't be angry." He gave a short chuckle and his arrogance returned. "I was doing you a favor. You're from this freakishly old-fashioned society and have no idea how modern women behave. Do you know how most girls act when they meet a guy like me? You should thank your lucky stars that I was willing to show you a good time before you become a farmer's wife and have to squeeze out a bunch of kids. No! You know what? You knew what you were doing coming here and I'm going to give you what you want!"

Terrified, Bethany spun around and reached for the lock on the door, but he grabbed her hand. She tried to pull it away. "Justin, no!"

"You want me as much as I want you."

"No, I don't." She tried to slide the lock out of the doorframe, but her fingers were shaking. "I want to go home."

"You're such a tease." Justin raised his voice as he pulled her hand away from the lock. He clutched her wrist in his fist, proving his strength.

She tried to move away and when he did not let her, she squeezed her eyes shut. Her voice trembled. "Don't—you can't do this—I'm with Everett."

"No, at the moment you're with me. You came to me in the middle of the night. That only means one thing."

She opened her eyes. "No. I came as your friend."

"You are not my friend. You're just a tease," he hissed.

"I don't know what you mean."

"You're not as innocent as you pretend to be."

Her quivering knees vibrated the fabric of her skirt. "I'm not pretending anything."

"Then you're an idiot." Justin let go of her. "I want you, but I'm not going to force you." He reached past her face and unlocked the door. Something dropped to the floor beside her and made a delicate clink, but she was too scared to look down. Justin's venomous gaze was full of disgust as he stepped back. "Stupid girl! Get out of here. Go back to your Quaker family and your sheep-loving boyfriend."

Bethany whirled out the door. She ran down the porch steps as Justin spat angry insults from the threshold. She was halfway to the road when she heard his door slam. A dog barked outside a village house on the other side of the graveyard. She choked on a sob as she wrapped herself in her coat and hurried home.

The cold air stung her face and neck, but her shaking fingers refused to button her coat collar. She tried to silence her weeping so as not to be heard while she sneaked home, but the trinity of fear, hurt, and regret unraveled the seams of her sensitive heart. Justin was wrong to grab her and kiss her, but he was right about one thing: she should not have gone to him.

Remorse gripped her, scraping her insides raw with self-loathing. She was an idiot. She should have listened to the people who loved her and she should have stayed away from Justin Mercer. Her visit to his home was not only a breach of their tradition but also had some universal meaning. The boundaries of cultural propriety were there for her protection. If her father found out, she would never outlive the shame she brought upon her family. If Everett found out, he might end their courtship before it began. Everett—she had barely thought of him when she was concerned for Justin. As she ran down the cobblestone street in the village to her family's property, she prayed Everett would never know of her blunder. Justin could leave and she could survive mourning his death, but the thought of losing Everett's affection was more than she could bear.

When the cobblestones ended at the edge of the village, Bethany walked through the grass beside the road to avoid making the gravel crunch beneath her feet. A low hum moved through the air to the west behind her. She looked up as a dark blur streaked across the sky overhead and soared toward the ocean. She saw two glowing fire-red rings behind the bird-shaped shadow and gasped. She focused on those two red circles, but it was out of sight before she took her next breath. Recalling Justin's description of the aircraft he flew, she raced to the house. She pushed the back door open and scurried through the dark kitchen and up the stairs. As she rounded the landing, she almost ran into Connor, who was standing in the hallway, holding the baby. He stepped back into the dimly lit nursery. "Bethany?"

"Connor, thank God," she panted. "There was an airplane. Did you hear it? I saw it. I think that's what it was. It had to be. It went toward the ocean—"

"An airplane?" Connor glanced at her coat. "Where?"

"Outside. Come quick. Maybe it will pass again."

He shifted Andrew into the crook of his arm and pointed at Bethany's closed bedroom door. "I thought you were asleep."

She shook her head as she noticed Connor's scowl. "Didn't you hear what I said? I saw an airplane fly over the village. An airplane!"

"Yeah, I heard you. What were you doing outside in the middle of the night?"

Lydia and Connor's bedroom door opened and Lydia stuck her head out. "What's going on?"

"Bethany says she saw an airplane," Connor answered Lydia while staring at Bethany.

Lydia walked out of their room and lifted her hands to take the baby. "I didn't hear anything. Connor, you told me airplanes are loud. Did you hear anything?"

"No," Connor said as he passed Andrew to Lydia. Then he slipped into their bedroom. "But I'll go check it out."

Bethany recalled the sensation she had felt as the aircraft passed above her. "It didn't make a loud noise—more of a hum. Maybe whatever is different in our atmosphere blocked the sound."

"That's an interesting hypothesis, Bethany, but now is not the time," Connor said from inside the bedroom.

Lydia looked at Bethany and angled her head. "Where have you been? It's not like you to go outside in the middle of a cold night."

"That's what I thought," Connor said as he came back out of their bedroom, wearing boots and his old flight jacket. He stood close to Bethany. "Please tell me you didn't go to see Justin?"

"It wasn't like that." Bethany answered louder than she intended. She did not want to talk about it at all, let alone where her father might hear. She lowered her voice. "It doesn't matter."

"It does matter," Lydia said as she moved close. Bethany felt trapped for the second time in a matter of minutes. She stepped back.

Connor zipped his jacket. "If there is something you need to confess, I want to hear it right now from you instead of later from Mercer. Be honest with me."

"We didn't do anything." Bethany had been caught in her blunder. She started to bury her face in her hands when she heard her father's door open.

"What has happened?" John asked, his concerned voice sounded low and sleepy.

Connor flipped his collar up around his neck and started down the stairs. "Bethany thinks she saw an airplane fly over the village. I'm going to check it out."

"An airplane?" John stepped into the hallway.

Andrew started fussing. Lydia carried the baby into the nursery and closed the door behind them.

Bethany glanced at her father. He loved her and trusted her and had no idea she had even left the house. She turned her face toward her bedroom door and could feel him looking at her through the dark.

"Are you dressed because you were about to leave, or are you just coming home?"

A lump rose in her throat. "Coming home," she whispered.

John did not respond. She waited for him to say something—anything—but he did not speak. Finally, he turned and went back into his bedroom. A few seconds later he came back out, buttoning his coat. "Go in your room and do not leave it until I come get you."

# Chapter Thirteen

I'm coming," Everett raised his voice as he shuffled to the front door. Levi and Mandy were waiting on the porch, backlit by the predawn sky. Everett yawned as he let them inside. "You're early. We were supposed to meet at the cairn after sunrise."

Levi walked in behind Mandy then closed the door. "Connor woke us. He said an airplane landed on the ship during the night."

"An airplane?" Everett rubbed his eye as he tried to process the news. Mandy sauntered past him and into the kitchen. He looked at Levi. "Is Mercer still leaving?"

"As far as we know." Levi's gaze was fixed on his wife. He crossed his arms. "Connor said for Mandy to stay here with your mother until we come back. Mandy knows what's going on, and she said she would take care of Roseanna if anything happens. Is your flock still sheltered?"

"Yes. James and Nicholas will stay with them." Everett ran his fingers through his hair. "Should I be worried?"

Levi shrugged. "Connor seemed concerned."

"When it comes to the outside world," Everett said as he walked back to his room, "Connor is always concerned."

In his room, Everett lifted his pants leg and strapped a sheathed hunting blade to his shin. Mandy clanked pans in the kitchen and Roseanna emerged from her bedroom. Levi began explaining the situation to Roseanna. Everett dropped his father's folding knife into one trouser pocket and a small scripture book into the other, and then he met Levi at the front door. "Let's go."

The clear sky warmed in color, but the air remained cold as Everett and Levi approached the village. They cut through the forest on the path near the Colburn property and trooped toward the cairn on the shore. When they were close, Everett saw Mercer ahead of them on the path. He nudged Levi and pointed. Levi's nostrils flared as he shook his head. He held up a hand in front of Everett, stopping him on the path. "Whatever happens, don't let him get to you."

"What do you mean?"

"I don't like him any more than you do, but you can't let him rile you like yesterday. He makes you angry and you lose focus—that's why you didn't block Connor's punch. I don't want to see that happen to you again."

Everett rubbed his cheek—now completely healed thanks to a layer of gray leaf salve overnight. "I'm not concerned with Mercer—it's Connor I'm worried about."

"Why? Connor is handling Mercer well." Levi contracted his brow. "Don't let Mercer make you doubt the people you know you can trust. And if he can't leave the Land, be careful you don't let him wreck your relationship with Bethany. He will try."

Everett grinned. "I've already won that battle. She picked me."

"Just be careful," Levi warned as they continued walking beneath the gray leaf trees to the shore. The sound of the waves increased as they came to the edge of the forest. John stood near the tall stack of stones that marked the place where the founders had arrived in the Land. Connor was bent over the backpack-style radio transmitter, demonstrating its use to Mercer. Though they were talking, Everett could not hear their words over the sound of the waves until he stepped close to the cairn. Mercer flipped several switches on the top panel of the green metal box. Then he closed the radio's lid, latched it, and hoisted it onto his back.

Connor lifted his chin acknowledging Levi and Everett's arrival. John turned and put his hand on Everett's shoulder. "Thank you for coming."

Everett nodded, then he looked at Connor. "What's this about an airplane landing on the ship?"

Connor sent John a look, then answered. "Late last night a jet was spotted flying over the village. It landed on the carrier. I've been out here ever since, watching for more activity, but it's still the only aircraft on the flight deck, and it hasn't moved since. We believe it had to be very close to the Land to be visible through the atmospheric phenomenon, but we won't know for certain until Mercer rows out and relays what he sees to us over the radio." Connor picked up their homemade receiver: a glass bottle coiled with magnet wire, nestled on a wood block with connections to a crystal diode and capacitor salvaged from the space debris. Everett's gaze followed an antenna wire to the top of the cairn and another wire that ran to a copper ground spike protruding from the nearby earth. Connor listened to the homemade speaker cup. "I'm not picking up any signals from the ship, so it's either farther away than it appears or the radio waves are blocked by whatever protects us."

Though fascinated by the science involved, Everett was more concerned with ensuring Mercer left the Land before he began transmitting signals. He looked at the ship on the horizon and shuddered. "Is it normal to have only one aircraft on a ship that big?"

"No," Connor answered. "At least it wasn't three years ago; I have no idea what's going on out there now. I think maybe the carrier is severely understaffed. Everyone is probably sick or dead. The sooner Lieutenant Mercer gets out there, the sooner we will find out." Connor glanced at Mercer, who was strapping on the radio pack. "The wind is calm right now, so that should make it easier."

"Good." Everett kept his voice level but his fists tightened as Mercer stepped away from the cairn.

Mercer made eye contact only with Connor. "Let's do this," he said as he walked through the group of men. He sent a shoulder into Everett on his way past. Everett took a slow breath and curled his toes inside his boots. He glanced at Levi. With one shake of his head, Levi reminded him to not respond to Mercer's vexation.

Connor and Mercer walked to a bright orange inflatable boat on the sand near the water. Everett and Levi followed, but John remained by the telescope and radio receiver. He lifted the receiver's wired cup to his ear, ready to listen.

Levi stopped on the dry sand, while Connor rolled up his pants legs and helped Mercer carry the boat into the water. As they neared the surf with the dinghy, Everett stepped close to Levi. "Connor is staying here, isn't he?"

"Of course," Levi answered. "He's just helping Mercer out to the sand bar. Believe me, Connor wants Mercer out of here as much as we do."

Everett felt a slight sense of relief. "I'm ready to see Mercer and his orange dinghy disappear over the horizon—so long as he doesn't bring an army back with him."

"He won't. I don't think he will even make it past the breakers without getting sucked into a current and thrown back to shore." Levi stared at the ocean. "We will be digging his grave by noon."

"Nothing would please me more," Everett mumbled.

Mercer stopped Connor and said something to him. Everett wondered why they had paused. He took a few steps closer to the water. Then Mercer, standing knee deep in the ocean, stuck his hand into his pocket and pulled something out. He looked back at Everett and raised his voice above the sound of the gentle waves. "By the way, your girlfriend left this at my place last night." He threw something and Everett caught the object reflexively. Everett opened his palm to see Bethany's silver bracelet. Anger burned in his gut as he traced his thumb over the little silver charm. He clenched his fist, burying the trinket in his hand, as he glared at Mercer. Mercer smirked and got in his dinghy. Furious, Everett lunged forward but Levi gripped his shoulders.

"Let him go," Levi growled. "It can't be true. Beth wouldn't do that. You know you can trust her. Don't let him get to you."

Everett's pulse rang in his ears as he watched Mercer paddle out to sea. "I want to kill him."

"The ocean will do it for you." Levi loosened his grip but did not let go.

Connor slogged out of the shallows and back onto the beach, glancing back at Mercer. Everett shook his shoulders free from Levi and marched toward Connor. As he held out the bracelet, he watched Connor's expression darken. Everett transferred all of the anger from Mercer to Connor. "You knew about this, didn't you?"

Connor glanced at the bracelet and then at Everett. "It wasn't like that. She just went to say goodbye to him."

"How do you know?" He stomped close, but Connor didn't flinch.

"Because she told me, and I believe her."

"Why didn't you tell me?"

"I knew what you would do and I couldn't allow that. I had to let him leave." Connor pointed at the sea. "Look, he's almost out of sight."

Everett looked at the horizon and saw the speck that he hoped would be his last glimpse of Justin Mercer. The rising sun's reflective rays forced Everett to look away. He stared at Bethany's bracelet—its delicate links embedded in the folds of his palm. He had been so afraid Connor would betray them, yet Connor had only been using diplomacy to secure their peace. The fire of Everett's anger cooled, but the fear of losing Bethany replaced it.

"Come on," Connor said as he walked away from the water's edge. "Let's go listen to the radio."

Stunned, Everett followed Connor and Levi to the cairn. His mind allowed no thought, save for the misery of imagining Bethany alone with another man and what that meant for their future—his future. He had spent ten days living through tormenting fear when she was in quarantine, but once she had accepted his offer of courtship, he no longer thought he would have to worry about her and Mercer. Now Mercer was gone and—just as Levi had warned—he had found a way to leave a rift between them. But it was not Mercer's fault alone—Bethany had gone to him.

When they got to the cairn, Connor bent over to unroll his pants cuffs and then brushed his hands together as he stood. "The waves are calmer than usual and there is hardly any current today. I think he's going to make it to the ship."

"That is good news," John said. He handed the speaker cup to Connor. "I have not heard any words yet, only a strange hissing sound."

Connor pressed the cup over one ear and plugged the other ear with his forefinger. He squinted out at the ocean as the men huddled around, awaiting his conveyance of Mercer's report. After a moment, Connor grinned. "He says he can see the ship."

Everett glanced out to sea but saw no trace of Mercer and his orange dinghy.

"He's getting close to the ship... the dinghy's outboard motor is still running... he said something changed in the air... the atmosphere around him changed... he said there is no land—he hoped to find land but there is no land." Connor glanced at John, "That was our signal. That means the Land is not visible." Then Connor squeezed his eyes shut. "It's getting harder to hear him... he's talking to someone else now. The ship's crew must have picked up his transmission, but I can't hear their signals. He's going to shoot a flare for them to see him." All the men looked toward the horizon, but saw nothing. "Dead air. He's outside of our atmosphere." Connor pulled the cup away from his ear. "That's it. He's gone."

John smiled and clapped once. "Hallelujah!"

"Maybe." Connor held up a finger as he looked at the ship. "Once the ship leaves, we will know we are safe."

"And if it doesn't leave?" Everett asked, his fear returning.

"We can only pray it does," John said as he bent to look through the telescope. "Connor, come take a look at this."

"What is it?" Levi asked.

Connor handed Everett the radio receiver as he put his eye to the telescope. "It's a storm and it is coming fast."

Everett looked out at the horizon and no longer saw the faint blur of the ship, but only a smudge of clouds. The wind increased and the air warmed as dark puffs began to billow over the horizon.

"We've seen this before," Levi said. "Let's get back to the house."

Connor knelt beside the telescope's tripod stand. He unhinged its legs and it collapsed into his arms. "I'm right behind you."

The incoming clouds suffocated the morning's light, leaving an eerie glow across the shore.

Everett watched as the waves' white caps lifted higher and higher from the sea. The encroaching water lapped over the footprints the men had left in the sand, and banks of foam began to push toward the cairn. "I thought the tide was going out this morning."

"It was," John replied as he tugged on Everett's sleeve. "Go to the house."

The incoming squall filled the air with sand, causing the men to shield their faces with their lapels as they hurried away from the shore. As Everett grabbed the antenna wire from the cairn, he shouted over the sound of the wind, "What about Mercer?"

No one replied. Everett hurried behind John and Connor as they followed Levi through the edge of the forest to the Colburn property. The wind whipped tree branches around them and threw sand at their backs. Connor laid the telescope at the doorstep as Levi and John fought the wind to close the shutters on the outside of the house. Everett left the radio receiver with the telescope and ran to help. He twisted the tiebacks beneath a heavy shutter on the guest room window and folded it into the casing. As he reached for the second shutter, Levi grabbed it. "I'll do this. You go lock all the shutters from the inside."

Everett held his hand over his face to block the wind as he ran to the Colburns' back door. When he stepped over the threshold, he wiped his boots on the mat, out of habit. The shutters clapped over the windows as John, Connor, and Levi closed them from the outside. Everett raced through the lower level of the Colburn house, lifting the sash windows and locking the shutters then lowering the windows. As he neared Isabella's room, Lydia appeared in the doorway. "Everett, what is happening?"

"It's a windstorm. It came in from the sea. The sky went from perfectly clear to completely filled with black clouds within minutes," he explained as he opened Isabella's window. He jerked the shutter's rusty lock into place and closed the window again.

"It is God's wrath," Isabella commented from her bed. "God controls who enters the Land and God judges those who try to leave."

Everett glanced at the elderly blind woman who was propped against a stack of pillows. He had not seen her in months. She looked frail and sallow—like Samuel had before he died.

Lydia stepped close to Isabella and took her hand. "There now, Aunt Isabella, I'm sure it is just a storm."

Everett had not meant to stare at Isabella. He felt rude and made himself look away. As he left the room he heard Lydia thank him for closing the shutters. He mumbled a response and, as he stepped into the hallway, Connor came around the stairs. "Thanks, Everett, I've got the rest."

Everett stopped in the hallway. Thunder cracked outside the house and shook the floor beneath his feet. He walked through the parlor and back into the kitchen. John and Levi were pulling off their boots and shedding their sandy overcoats. Bethany was probably upstairs in her bedroom. He wanted to go to her, to demand an explanation, to beg her to say it was not true, but the sooner he saw her, the sooner their relationship would end. He did not want to lose her; after losing his father, it would be too much to bear, but if she had been unfaithful in courtship, he would have little choice. He slid his hand into his pocket and felt her silver bracelet.

John brushed his palms together and asked Levi, "Is Mandy with Roseanna?" When Levi gave a quick nod, John looked at Everett. "I think you both should stay here until the storm passes. There is no sense in going out in that."

Everett's mother was safe at home and the animals were safe in the barn; he was the only one in danger, having his heart sliced open by a silver trinket. As he thought of Mercer's parting words, he wondered if he even knew Bethany at all. He remembered Levi's warning and did not want to fall victim to a lie, but his fear would be neither relieved nor confirmed until he spoke to Bethany.

John walked out of the kitchen. "Excuse me gentlemen, there is something I need to take care of."

Everett sat at the table as he heard John climb the stairs. He looked at Levi. "Does your father know what Mercer accused Bethany of?"

"I don't live here anymore, so I don't know any more than you do," Levi said as he picked up the radio receiver and started to tinker with the wire. "But if he doesn't know, I'd say he's about to find out."

* * *

Justin Mercer unstrapped the radio from his back and allowed it to drop into the ocean before he grabbed the helicopter's rescue hoist and was pulled from the dinghy. Once inside the helicopter, he stared back toward the Land. He had lost sight of it after rowing out only a few hundred feet from shore, and with the storm between them and the Land, it was hidden from the crew also. Black clouds billowed behind them while the rescue helicopter carried him to the platform. The storm rose like smoke from a volcano as if the sea intended to keep the Land undetectable—even from him as he approached the carrier. Mercer didn't care about the cause of the storm or the cause of the Land's disappearance. He had promised to take his experience in the Land to his grave, and now all he wanted was to get back to his old life.

With a synthetic fleece first aid blanket wrapped over his wet shoulders, Mercer followed the aviation rescue swimmer through one of the carrier's stale corridors. It was good to be back on a platform, even though the ship was eerily quiet.

The rescuer glanced back as he spoke over his shoulder. "You've been on a dinghy for a month, and you look healthier than most of our crew."

Mercer scowled and rubbed his whiskered jaw. It was not a month's worth of stubble, but it was enough to make him look ragged. "The weather was favorable until today. I guess I got lucky, that's all."

"Luck and a water filter and a fishing line," the rescuer laughed.

Mercer wanted to laugh too, but he feigned lightheadedness instead, hoping to portray an exhausted victim. He slowed his pace and received a sympathetic look from the rescuer. "It must have been awful. You were smart to stay off the icebreaker while the other men died."

"Are they all dead?" Mercer asked, thinking of Volt.

"Yes," the rescuer kept talking as he turned a corner and opened a door for Mercer. "We found four bodies and a lot of old equipment— not as old looking as that radio you had strapped to your back when we found you. Good thing you used it though. There is nothing but water out here for hundreds of miles."

Mercer nodded. "Yeah, nothing at all."

# Chapter Fourteen

Bethany lifted her head from her feather pillow and listened to the wind howl outside the sturdy old house. As she drew her legs from under the warm quilt, she reached to straighten her nightgown, but instead of feeling its thin cotton, she felt the sweaty velvet of the red dress she had fallen asleep in. The memories of the night's events flooded back, and with them the aching burden of her family's disappointment.

The wind's groan increased, and Bethany went to her bedroom window to look out. She peeled back the lace-trimmed curtain, and then gasped when she saw the trees in front of the house bending and buckling in the violent wind. A limb cracked off a dormant fruit tree, and sprigs of latent buds flew past her window. She pushed her hands against the glass and looked far to one side then to the other and saw her father closing the storm shutters outside the parlor window below. Dark clouds roiled through the morning sky, turning its soft pink into a smutty black. It was a rainless storm from a furious sky. She gripped the curtains and yanked them together, protecting herself from the disturbing visual.

Bethany backed toward her bed. The only other time she had witnessed a storm so severe was when Luke and Walter were killed at sea. Levi had stayed with her during that horrible storm, and Everett had comforted her when she grieved the loss of her friends. But now she was alone, having been ordered to stay in her room until her father came for her. She hoped he would hurry inside and come get her, even though when he did it would be to reprimand her for her foolish breach of custom.

Something hit Bethany's window, making her jump. She scurried onto her bed and leaned into the headboard. If Justin had rowed out at sunrise like he planned, he might be drowning in the ocean. She hugged her pillow and wrapped her legs beneath the quilt, trying not to imagine the panicked fright of being pulled into a raging current. No matter how he had hurt her, she still did not want him to suffer.

The walls creaked with the changing air pressure brought by the storm. Bethany heard the men talking downstairs and wished her father would come get her. If anything else hit the window, it might shatter the glass and she would be exposed to the storm's violence. She tried to listen to the voices, but could not discern their words for the sound of the wind.

Quick stomps ascended the stairs. As she looked at her door, lightning cracked outside the window, increasing her fear. "Father?" Bethany yelled.

The door opened. "I am here."

"Oh, Father—" She pushed her pillow away and started to move to the edge of the bed but noticed his scowl and wind-tossed hair. She froze as she remembered his last words to her during the night. Instead of going to him, she slunk back against the headboard and pulled the pillow to her chest. She wanted him to tell her to come downstairs with the family, but he only stepped into her bedroom and closed the door.

Tears of compunction slid down Bethany's cheeks. She could not look her father in the eye, so she wiped her cheek against the pillow and turned her face to the window. "Isn't it dangerous to be upstairs during a storm?"

"I am with you." John stepped close to the bed then stopped. "Look at me."

"No. I know you're angry."

"I am not angry with you, Bethany. I am disappointed."

"That's worse." Bethany's hand trembled as she dragged a knuckle beneath her eye, catching a fresh tear. She never wanted to disappoint anyone, least of all her father.

"We need to talk about what happened last night."

"I only went to say goodbye."

"You went alone to visit a man in the middle of the night."

Though she had her reasons—and they had seemed paramount at the time—she felt foolish now. Bethany swallowed, trying to relieve the lump in her throat. "To say goodbye," she reiterated.

"You broke the rules. You disobeyed." Thunder vibrated the house, but John's deep voice never wavered in its calm authority. "You are an adult and you can make your own decisions, but you also must understand what is at stake now—"

"I just wanted Justin to know that one person here cared about him."

"I told you not to go. Connor told you to stay away from Justin. Lydia warned you too, and I am sure you knew Everett's feelings on the matter. We all warned you—not to keep you from something good—but to protect you because we love you." When Bethany took a breath to defend herself, John raised a palm and continued. "And we did not tell you as adults instructing a child, but as adults helping another adult. Just because you were the last person in this family to reach adulthood does not mean you are still a child. This is not an issue of age but of wisdom. We could all see you were being tempted to cross a boundary with serious consequences and we wanted to help you. But you were so worried about what Justin thought and felt that you went after his approval. Did you get it?"

Bethany looked up at her father. His probing questions pierced her heart with truth. "No, I only got hurt."

"The surest way to get hurt is to seek the approval of the godless." John's brow furrowed and he sat on the bed near Bethany. "What happened?"

"Nothing."

"Tell me the truth." When Bethany remained silent, John blew out a breath. "Bethany, if a man wants to marry you someday, according to our tradition, as your father I will have to attest that you are pure—"

"I am," Bethany blurted out, as she grabbed her father's arm. "He didn't… we didn't… he kissed me and I left. That was it, I promise."

John nodded slowly and folded his hands. "It sounds like Justin thought you went see to him for the same reason we all did."

Everyone seemed to know something she did not. She wanted to blame growing up without a mother for her lack of understanding, but she remembered the constant admonitions from the people who cared about her. There had been no lack of guidance, only a lack of trust on her part. Bethany drew her lips into her mouth and nodded. "I had to find out for myself."

"That is normal for a person your age." John glanced at her and continued. "I know you sometimes question the validity of our traditions, but I hope you see our boundaries exist to protect us. You are free to live as you choose and cross those boundaries if you wish. And if you live that way, we will still love you and we will forgive you, but we will stop warning you. Eventually, you will find yourself unprotected and isolated. By crossing boundaries last night, you hurt yourself and you hurt people who love you."

Bethany inched away from the headboard and closer to her father. He wrapped an arm behind her back, and she was relieved to feel his love and forgiveness, but the possibility of the rest of her family being hurt or suspicious of her kept the knot tight in her throat. She looked at her hands. "I'm sorry—truly I am."

"I forgive you."

"I want the others to forgive me too."

"Lydia and Connor will not hold this against you. Everett is a good man and he will forgive you too, but whether or not he will still want to court you—I cannot say. His honor is at stake."

The thought of Everett rejecting her for one stupid mistake hit Bethany with gut-churning force. She looked to her father. "Please speak to him for me."

"You are an adult now; I am not going to punish you, but I am not going to fix your mistakes either. Your choice hurt your relationships. Only you can make it right."

"How do I fix this?"

John sighed. "Bethany, you have a sensitive heart—you get that from your mother. I am sorry you had to grow up without her, but you have never gone a day without the guidance of people God has placed in your life. Go to them and tell them what you told me: that you regret your actions and your purity was spared. They need to know you appreciate their help and you regret not listening to them. As you get older and your choices affect your place in the community, you will want to have people like Lydia and Connor, Levi and Mandy, and Roseanna and Everett—people who are wise and will advise you to live in a way that honors your family and your creator. This family and this village—they are your true inheritance. Levi has chosen his own inheritance. Connor, who was grafted into our family providentially, will probably inherit the position of village overseer one day. Everett has inherited his father's property and position among the elders. I know it is different for you being the youngest daughter in that you will not inherit physical possessions, but these people are your inheritance. You must treat them as such."

Bethany gave a small chuckle as she examined her cuticles. "Actually, Father, I will have an inheritance of my own."

"Oh?"

"Mrs. Vestal would like to leave me the pottery yard." She waited for her father's reaction. "If that is acceptable to the elders, of course. No one in her family has interest in it, and she says I am the best potter she's ever known."

John leaned back and pressed his palms into the mattress. "I will discuss it with the elders when Mrs. Vestal presents the details to us, but it sounds like a good plan to me."

"Really?" Bethany ignored the wind's moan outside the window and smiled. "Thank you, Father."

"Just do not forget your heritage—your family, the village, and our values. Whether you have a family of your own to pass your heritage to some day or spend your life shaping lumps of clay into beautiful vessels, always protect your true inheritance."

* * *

Bethany stayed close to her father as she followed him down the stairs and into the kitchen. Though it was morning, the shuttered windows made the downstairs rooms as dark as night. Flames flickered inside the globes of two lanterns on the kitchen table, and the gray leaf log in the fireplace added a soft glow to the room. As John stepped to the side, Bethany saw the people she loved and had hurt. Connor leaned back in his seat and furrowed his brow like he did in the classroom when he was waiting for a naughty student to explain bad behavior. Levi appeared impassive, but he emanated disappointment, bearing evidence of his knowledge of her foolish choice. Everett sat at the far end of the table in her father's usual seat. He had his head in his hands and did not look at her. Bethany wished her father would speak for her, but when he put his hand at her back and nudged her closer to the table, she knew there was no way out of it. She began to pick at her nails then looked up when Lydia walked into the room behind them.

Lydia passed her and glanced in the bassinet in the corner of the room. "Andrew is sound asleep and Aunt Isabella says she wants to stay in her room and nap." The wind banged the shutters against the kitchen window. "How either of them can be at peace during this ruckus is beyond me." Lydia looked at the men and then at Bethany. "Oh, am I interrupting?"

John motioned to the empty chair beside Connor. "Have a seat, Lydia. Bethany has something she needs to say."

Bethany felt her knees quiver and shifted her weight. She swallowed and looked at Connor.

"You saved my life when I caught that horrible illness and then you worked so hard to protect me. I didn't listen to you and I'm sorry." She moved her gaze to Lydia. "You tried to warn me too. I should have listened and I'm sorry I didn't." A small smile curved the corner of Lydia's mouth and she nodded. Bethany looked at Levi. "I know you were worried about me and I only made it worse. I'm sorry." Levi grinned and the light hit his eyes, relieving her, though she already knew he would easily forgive her.

Everett lifted his head and raked both hands through his hair. Though his jaw was shadowed with whiskers, it was the darkness in his eyes that made him look harsh. When his gaze met hers, Bethany wanted to look away, but she forced herself to carry on. This was some rite of passage, some test of development, or one of those maturing experiences her father so often referred to, and she would not back down. She straightened her spine. "Everett, you made your wishes very clear and I went against them. I understand why you are upset and I'm so sorry." He did not move. His gaze was intense, so Bethany looked at the others to continue her apology. "I hope my foolish actions haven't brought shame to my family, and I hope you all will forgive me."

Lydia stood and embraced Bethany. "Of course, we forgive you."

As Lydia backed away, Connor smiled. "Yeah, Beth, you're forgiven."

Bethany glanced at Levi and he smiled at her. Everett was still staring at her. He had not yet offered forgiveness. She was too nervous to let him catch her eye. He stood and everyone looked at him and then at her. Everett turned to John. "May I speak with Bethany alone?"

"Of course." John held an open hand toward the parlor.

Everett passed Bethany without touching her. Lydia and Connor exchanged a sad look then Lydia pressed her palm to her stomach. For once Bethany felt like she knew what they knew, and she pined for her former ignorance.

Her heart broke a little more with each step as she followed Everett into the dim, empty parlor. Her family had forgiven her and she felt their love. She wished they would follow her and stand with her as she endured the rejection of the man she loved, but she had to face him alone.

Everett stepped to the fireplace. He stared at the burning log on the grate as he leaned his forearm upon the mantel. Bethany sat on the edge of the divan, her body so tense it could have sustained the position without a seat below her. Gusting wind rattled the shutters outside the parlor windows, producing an eerie commotion that made her wish the whole hopeless debacle would soon end so she could begin mourning the loss of Everett's love. She wanted to speak, to beg his forgiveness, to make a cute remark or a joke or a compliment—anything to regain his approval—but instinct told her to remain silent while he formed his thoughts; if a man had something true and raw to say, it was best not to interrupt the process and risk silencing what he most needed—yet least wanted—to say.

Everett turned from the fire and sank his hands into his trouser pockets. As Bethany wondered if he still carried the little scripture book, he drew one hand out and opened his palm, revealing her silver bracelet. She stared at the vase-shaped charm and remembered the sound it made when it fell from her wrist at Justin's cabin the night before. She'd been too scared of Justin's desire to look at the floor then, and she was too scared of Everett's rejection to look at his face now.

Everett stepped close to the divan and held the bracelet out to her. "Is it true? Did you go to him last night?"

Bethany swallowed and took the bracelet. "Yes."

"What happened?"

"I only wanted to let him know someone here cared about him. I couldn't get the image of Luke and Walter's drowning out of my mind, and I had to warn him about the sea." She felt a surge of emotion and tried to keep her voice quiet, knowing Isabella was asleep and the others were probably trying to listen from the kitchen. "I was afraid he was being driven away and I needed to know it was his choice to leave."

"What happened?"

"I walked to his cabin and told him those very things. He said he wanted to leave the Land and he knew how to survive the water." Thunder rumbled and Bethany cringed. "He said he would be fine."

"I don't care about any of that, Bethany." Everett said her name through clenched teeth. "This is the last time I will ask you: what happened?"

"Justin said he knew why I really went to him and he grabbed me." She struggled to form the words. "He kissed me roughly and poorly. When I told him not to, he let me go, and then he said some terrible things."

Everett wiped both hands across his face but it did little to remove his angry expression. "I have waited my whole life to kiss you and—if I had—it would have been neither rough nor poor. I would have spoken kindly to you all of your days."

"I'm so sorry." She blurted out then recoiled as Everett silently turned back to the fire. If he could not forgive her now, maybe he would in time, but she could not think beyond the present torturous moment. The pain in her chest felt watery and cold. If anything had caused it other than him, she would have gone to Everett for comfort. While her fingers felt along the silver links of the bracelet, she longed for her mother—the woman she barely remembered but was constantly compared to. Everyone said she was sensitive like her mother, emotionally intuitive like her mother, tenderhearted like her mother. Why could she not fix this like her mother?

She watched Everett's slumped shoulders and wondered if his anger against her would ever dissipate. At once, she realized it was not anger she sensed from him at all. "You're not mad—you are afraid."

Everett straightened his shoulders and turned on his heel. "I didn't say that."

"You didn't have to." A flash of lightning sprayed a virescent glow through the cracks in the shutters, but Bethany did not flinch.

"Then how do you know?"

"I can feel it."

"Of course you can." Everett gave a small chuckle but not a happy one. He walked back to the divan and sat on the arm, retaining his position over her. "You're right: I am afraid. Beth, I lost my father and nearly lost you in the same day. And then within a day of entering courtship with me, you go to another man." When she opened her mouth, Everett put his hands up. "I know you had your reasons and you regret it, but it makes me afraid that I will easily lose you. I forgive you, but if I am going to build a life with you, I need to be able to trust you."

"If by trust you mean assurance that I will be faithful to you, then yes, be assured my heart is yours. But if by trust you mean assurance that I will not make mistakes then no, you cannot trust me because I will fail you. I'm only human. And so are you—you will fail me too." She shifted toward him. "You're right to be afraid—this is scary. Our hearts and our futures are at stake. I'm afraid too."

Everett blew out a breath and lowered himself to the cushion beside her. He put his arm across the back of the divan. "This is one of those opportunities for me to love you through it, isn't it?"

"I hope so." Bethany released a long breath and grinned slightly. "But if you don't, I will love you through that too."

"You've changed."

"How so?"

"You're starting to speak like a Colburn."

"That is the highest compliment I've ever received."

When the shutters on both sides of the room clattered in the wind, Bethany leaned against Everett's side. She could feel the gentle movement of his chest with his breath. "How will we know when we are safe?"

"From each other or from the outside world?" he asked. She could tell he was smiling and pulled away to look at him. He grinned at her and then continued. "Mercer made it out to sea before the storm blew in. He was speaking to Connor over the radio and said that he went through the change in the atmosphere and could no longer see the Land. Connor heard him speaking to the ship's rescue workers before we lost signal. Connor said we are safely hidden within our atmosphere, but we will know for certain that the danger is over once the ship is gone."

"Do you think Justin is safe?"

"Connor said it was an American ship and whoever Mercer was talking to, he sounded pleased. They probably rescued him."

"What if the storm got to him before they did?"

"Connor thinks Mercer is safe. I trust Connor."

Bethany did too, but her fear remained. She wanted to know she could depend on Everett's strength. "If Justin's body washes back to shore like Luke and Walter's did, it might break me."

Everett pulled her close to his side and she laid her head against his shoulder. "I've known you since the day you were born," he said. "We've been through a lot together. Have I ever let you break alone?"

"No, never once."

"I plan to keep that up for the next—I don't know—seventy years or so."

Bethany closed her eyes as she breathed in the hope of a future with him. "And I will let you."

"When we go out after the storm, if you find a reason to break, you can break in my arms. But if we go out and find a reason to celebrate, we will celebrate together." His voice sounded low and sure. "I waited so long to court you and then all this happened. As soon as it's over, I'll hire as many men as I have to so that I can spend time with you. We can do whatever you want: picnics on the bluffs, strolls along the beach, or you can curl your hair and I'll parade you through the village."

Bethany hummed. "Yes—all of it."

"What would you like to do first? Anything you want."

"Anything?"

"Yes."

"I would like to spend a day working with you on your farm."

Everett pulled his head back a degree and contracted his brows. "My farm?"

She nodded. "The pottery yard is closed for the winter, I don't have school anymore, and Lydia takes care of everything around here. I'd really like to see the animals and see what life is like on your farm."

A wild grin spread across Everett's face. "You just made me the happiest man in the village. Very well, it's a date."

\* \* \*

Everett relaxed with his head against the back of the overstuffed armchair in the Colburns' parlor. As he watched the warm glow of the burning gray leaf log upon the grate, he listened to the pleasant feminine voices coming from the kitchen. Though Bethany and Lydia's conversation was undecipherable because of the din produced by the rainless storm outside, Everett absorbed every note of Bethany's laugh as she helped Lydia prepare their lunch. Over the course of the morning hours, sheltered in the Colburn house, Everett's complete forgiveness had sprouted a desire to spend his life leading Bethany in love. She no more wanted a controller than he wanted to control, but she was used to the strong guidance of her father and would not respect a husband who lacked the ability to shepherd his family with wisdom.

Everett glanced at the three other men who were lounging in the parlor. He and Levi were both raised under John's capable leadership, and Connor came to the Land already possessing the seven virtues; they were all bound by their desire to live by a noble and ancient code. And at present, they were confined indoors as a violent storm battered their village.

Levi was reclined lengthwise on the divan, staring at the ceiling. Connor was sitting cross-legged on the rug with his infant son lying beside him; a stream of drool connected Andrew's chin to the rug as he pushed himself up and attempted to crawl. John shifted his body in his chair when the old clock on the wall behind him clicked into the noon position. He looked at the fire beside him and propped his heels on a wooden footstool. Though the outside shutters vibrated in non-rhythmic pulses, and sand and twigs continuously sprinkled against the house, Everett felt content. He was at peace with Bethany and, therefore, his world made sense.

At once, a strange silence shrouded the room. Glints of the noonday light spilled between the slats on the shutters, sending a field of parallel shadows across the baby's back. The chair's stiff fabric crackled as Everett lifted his head. John craned his neck to look at the covered window behind his chair. Levi arose from his reclined position on the divan; he put his feet to the floor and raised both eyebrows. In one motion, Connor scooped Andrew from the rug and stood. "It's over!" Connor said as he carried the baby into the kitchen.

Everett followed John as the men rushed to the back door and tugged on their boots. The sun's light blinked between the dissipating clouds and sparkled off the sand that was strewn throughout the yard. Everett rubbed his hands together as he walked into the calm but cold air outside.

In silence, they surveyed the damage. Broken tree limbs, downed fence, and a drift of sand and sea foam piled against the east side of the house and the cottage. The barn appeared to be undamaged, but a chorus of nervous whinnies and moos attested to the state of the anxious animals locked inside. Everett's concern for his flock grew and he wanted to get back to his farm. At last, John returned from his perambulation and instructed the men. "Connor, Everett, go and check the shore. Levi and I will walk through the village."

Everett nodded and followed Connor to the house to get the telescope. As soon as they walked inside the back door, Lydia began pelting Connor with questions. Everett lifted his coat from the hook behind the door and looked at Bethany. She watched him with wide eyes as her hand stirred a ladle in a pot of stew. He shrugged on his coat and stepped close to her. "Connor and I are going to the shore. Stay inside until one of us comes back and tells you it's safe. Please. Whatever we find out there, I'll handle it a lot better if I know you are safe in here. I will come back and tell you everything, I promise. Just stay here for now."

Bethany let go of the ladle and it swirled once inside the rim of the caldron. She reached a hand to his coat and smoothed his lapel. "I will wait." She grinned. "But not indefinitely. My curiosity cannot be restrained for long."

"Fair enough." Everett began to grin at her but stopped when he realized it might be the last time he saw her. He did not know what would be waiting for him on the shore—possibly Mercer's dead body, or worse, an invading army. He quickly tried to memorize how she looked in that moment. Then Connor called to him from outside, so Everett squeezed Bethany's hand and left the Colburn house.

Broken branches and sticky seaweed littered the forest path. Everett walked in front of Connor, pulling the most obtrusive limbs out of their way as they trudged to the shore. Connor cradled the telescope in his arms, and his brow creased with worry. As they neared the beach, Everett pointed to the cairn. "Look at that—not a stone out of place."

Connor nodded. "When the founders built something, they did it right."

While Connor set up the telescope, Everett walked on and surveyed the shore. The beach's white sand was spotted with clumps of kelp, broken coral, and dead fish. The storm had spewed putrid froth on the shore, and it bubbled in thick ribbons all the way to the bluffs. Waves still came in rapid swells, breaking high over the sand bar. The damage sullied the natural beauty of the coast, leaving a residue that could be cleaned from the Land sooner than the image would be cleared from his mind.

Everett walked farther down the coast and saw no sign of Mercer or his little orange boat, only seaweed and sludge. He hiked back to the cairn, then he turned and scanned the horizon. The light blue of the clearing sky touched the dark blue of the sea in unbroken parallel. He looked at Connor. "No sign of Mercer and I can't see the ship. Can you?"

"Hang on…" Connor adjusted the telescope and squinted through the eyepiece. "No, it's gone." He stood and grinned. "The ship is gone."

"The ship is gone!" Everett repeated, confirming the fact to himself. "Do you think Mercer made it to the ship before it left?"

Connor's smile faded and he shielded his eyes from the sun as he cast his gaze out to sea. "Yeah, I do. I think the storm was localized inside the atmosphere close to shore. Even if it wasn't, the rescue swimmers would have hoisted him out of the water before the storm had a chance to touch him." He shrugged and bent back to the telescope. "The ship is gone and the Land is safe."

Everett stared at the unblemished horizon and felt every ounce of his fear dissolve. A laugh escaped his throat. He wanted to celebrate, but not without Bethany. He glanced back at Connor. "I've got to go," he said as he jogged to the forest path. "I've got a life waiting for me."

# Chapter Fifteen

Bethany dragged a heavy bucket of nails across the ground behind her trading table. Only an hour into the weekly village market and her pottery stock was almost depleted. As the crowd momentarily thinned near her booth, she removed her shawl and tossed it over a bushel of early spring vegetables, which she had acquired by trade of a single ceramic bud vase.

As she turned back around, Roseanna Foster stopped in front of the pottery booth. Roseanna looked like her old self, having opted for a soft yellow blouse tucked into a skirt the color of the silvery new growth on the gray leaf trees instead of her black mourning dress. She beamed at Bethany and held up a new pair of gloves. "The leather man is here from Riverside. I got these for Everett. He always misplaces his work gloves. You'd better get over there if you want any leather. It'll be gone soon."

Bethany motioned to the back of her booth where four pair of work gloves lay atop a new leather satchel. "I traded with him earlier this morning."

"So I see." Roseanna's eyes widened. "And half the other merchants too, by the looks of it."

"People need dishes." Bethany grinned as she rearranged the last three remaining pottery pieces on her trading table. She slid the largest bowl to the center. "And I have a horse to buy."

"You've got a knack for business, that's for sure, but why go to all this trouble when Everett has plenty of horses? They'll be yours too once you marry."

"Not really." Bethany wiped a speck of dust from the dark blue glaze of the bowl then looked at Roseanna. "Besides, I want to spend my life with Everett because I love him, not because I need his possessions."

"I felt the same way about Samuel when I married him, though I wasn't a craftsman like you. I had nothing to trade to make my own living. I was simply a farm girl who loved to take care of home and garden and babies. I still do." Roseanna's smile relaxed slightly. "Everett won't talk about it, but I know he'll be asking you to marry soon."

"Missus—I mean—Roseanna, Everett and I talk about marriage all the time. It won't be a surprise when he asks me because he is waiting for me to tell him when I am ready."

Roseanna raised a hand and her ruffled cuff slid to her forearm. "I hope you're not waiting on my account. I love taking care of my home, but you'll be the lady of the house when you and Everett marry. It is his inheritance and that's the way it has been done in the Foster family for generations. Samuel's mother took to her room when I came into the house. I doubt I'll be able to do that, but perhaps you won't mind if I take to the garden." When Bethany tilted her head and smiled, Roseanna continued. "Then again, if you continue your work at the pottery yard, you might need me around the house… maybe you'll need my help with the children too."

"I will need your help." Bethany sensed Roseanna's need for reassurance. She nodded. "Very much."

Roseanna reached across the table and laid her hand on Bethany's arm. "I'm proud of you, sweet girl. And your mother would have been proud of you too." She pointed to the stack of trade behind the table. "Surprised but proud."

As the crowd shifted, Bethany noticed Everett speaking with a trader on the other side of the busy open-air market. Roseanna turned too. "Is that the silversmith Everett is talking to? They seem to be negotiating, but whatever for?" She put her hand over her heart. "Oh, I see. Yes, well, I suspect he will be getting your father's permission soon. And he'll probably want Levi and Connor's blessing too, knowing how protective those boys are of you."

Bethany smiled. "No—he's had their blessing for years."

Everett shook the trader's hand then turned and walked through the crowd toward Bethany. Roseanna said something about going to look at cloth and walked away. Bethany glanced at her and mumbled a goodbye, then she looked back at Everett. His lips were pursed like he was whistling, but she couldn't hear the tune over the sound of the villagers and the merchants and the children. A gust of wind blew a cloud of loose white petals from a nearby fruit tree through the market. The breeze mixed with the gray leaf's scent and the salty ocean air, producing the sweet fragrance of springtime in the Land. A group of children ran in front of Everett. He smiled at them and continued walking with his gaze fixed on Bethany as he approached the pottery booth.

She finally heard the notes he was whistling as she stepped around the table to meet him. He stopped his song and drew her into his arms. She pulled back, excited to tell him about her morning, but he held her against his chest for one more heartbeat before he released her. Bethany smiled and looked up at him. "What is that tune you were whistling?"

Everett flipped his hair off his forehead. "Just a song I've been working on these past few months."

"Is it ready?"

"Almost." He held her hand in his and glanced at her finger. "How about you? Are you ready?"

Bethany grinned. "Almost."

Everett looked behind him when Roseanna's cackle of a laugh rang from across the market. She had both hands clasped to her face as she chatted with a group of women near the cloth trader's booth. Everett turned back to Bethany. "It's good to see her being herself again."

"Yes, it is."

Everett rubbed his thumb over Bethany's knuckles as he held her hand. "She is afraid we won't need her."

Bethany nodded. "I know. I assured her we would."

"Thank you." He kissed her hand then released it and motioned to the merchandise behind her table. "I see you've been busy this morning."

She glanced at the pile: leather items, buckets of nails, bolts of cloth, baskets of food, and a shovel. "I'm taking it to Mark Cotter for the horse after I trade these last three pieces."

Everett picked up the bowl in the center of the table. "I'll trade you one arthritic herding dog for this."

She lowered her chin and affected her voice with a masculine tone. "I'm sorry, sir, I have no use for an arthritic herding dog."

"Very well," His face drew into a serious expression then a smile threatened his affectation. "I see you are a shrewd negotiator. How about four hundred ewes and a highly domestic mother?"

"All that for a bowl?" She snorted.

"Never mind, I don't want the bowl after all." They both laughed. When their chuckles died out, Everett rocked back on his heels. He was quiet for a moment and glanced around the marketplace. Then he looked back at her and pointed to the trade stacked behind her. "If you insist on buying your own horse, will you at least let me handle the trade for you?"

"No, thank you."

"Will you let me accompany you then?"

"Fine. You may go with me." Bethany held up a finger. "But you'd better let me do the talking."

Everett grinned. "It's a deal."

\* \* \*

Bethany nestled her bare feet in the powdery white sand, then she leaned down and traced their outline with her finger. As Everett fed the bonfire with a fresh load of dried branches, a log popped, sending sparks high above the flames. Bethany coolly looked up, brushed the sand from her fingertips, and smiled at him. Everett grinned and resumed his kindling.

"Am I too late?" Lydia called as she stepped out of the darkened forest path and onto the beach.

"We were just getting started," Connor answered from the end of the log bench. "How is Mr. Roberts?"

Lydia's fire-lit face looked exhausted. "He will be fine. Thirty-two stiches. I wouldn't normally divulge a patient's details, but he was so proud to live through being gored in the shoulder by a bull that he wanted you men to know the stitch count as if it were some sign of masculinity." She lowered herself to the log and sat beside Connor. Then she leaned forward to look past Bethany and Mandy at Levi. "Oh, and Mrs. Roberts said to tell you she is waiting for you to build the new cabinetry in her kitchen."

Levi shrugged. "I've already told her twice: I will get to it as soon as I've finished the addition on our house." Mandy smiled and reclined against him. He put his palm across her abdomen. His splayed hand covered most of her pregnant belly.

Bethany watched Levi's hand on Mandy's stomach. Something happened inside the enigmatic bump and Mandy and Levi both laughed.

"She kicked!" Mandy said.

"He kicked," Levi corrected, grinning.

"There is no way to know until the big day—not in the Land anyway," Connor interjected. "Except with Andrew—I knew he was a boy."

"After he was born," Lydia laughed. "I think most men hope there firstborn is a boy."

"Not me." Everett sat on the empty slice of log beside Bethany then wrapped his arm around her. "I don't care either way."

Bethany glanced at the thin silver band around her finger—a promise ring, he had called it when he gave it to her—a custom Connor encouraged due to their lengthy courtship. The newness of the silver reflected the firelight. She turned her face into Everett's neck. "You don't care if your first child is a boy or a girl?"

she asked in a near whisper, but it still drew curious glances.

Everett moved his hand to the small of her back and looked at the others. "I have two hundred fourteen lambs in the flock right now… I'll be happy to have anything born without cloven hooves."

Mandy laughed again; it sounded like music. Then she flinched. "That was a big one! Feel it, Bethany."

Levi removed his hand and Bethany laid hers across Mandy's middle. She felt the stirring of the child beneath the thin cotton fabric of Mandy's summer dress and it made her wish for the same—someday. She imagined what it must be like to feel a child growing inside and wondered if she would sense her own child's emotions from the womb.

Mandy smiled at her. "It's amazing, isn't it?"

Levi leaned forward and looked at Connor. "Tell us a story."

Connor chuckled while Lydia and Mandy groaned about not wanting to be frightened. Levi encouraged Connor to make the story shocking, but Mandy complained gory stories made her nauseated. Everett traced his finger across Bethany's back, spelling out letters no one else could see: I-L-O-V-E. She stared at the fire and the sounds of her siblings and their spouses dissipated as she focused on Everett's furtive message: Y-O-U. Even in the middle of the group, he found a private way to make a connection. She pulled her hand away from Mandy's belly and leaned into Everett's side. He pressed his lips against the top of her head as he drew more letters on her back. She felt safe with him, cherished and settled.

Connor patted the air with his hand, quieting Mandy and Lydia. "Okay, have you heard the one about the guy…"

# Epilogue

Justin Mercer tucked in his shirt and fastened his belt, then began packing his few personal possessions into an oversized duffle bag. After spending his nights alone in the musty, eight-man stateroom, and his days attempting sundry maintenance procedures aboard the eerily understaffed aircraft carrier, he was ready to disembark as soon as they were harbored at Norfolk. He gave the room one last glance, then double-checked the duffle bag for the only item he cared about—a sock filled with a dozen seeds from the gray leaf tree. As he untied the sock and looked inside at the marble-sized seeds, he wondered how and where he would plant them so the miraculous trees would grow safely in America while he returned to duty. He remembered the greenhouse planters his mother used during winter months and considered building something similar.

A knock echoed through his door, jarring him from his thoughts. "On my way," Mercer blurted as he retied the sock and buried it in the duffle bag. After a glance at his wristwatch, Mercer lifted the bag to his shoulder. He left the room, walked the narrow corridor to a flight of stairs then through another corridor, and entered the ready room where a commander awaited him.

"Your reenlistment has been approved," the commander said before Mercer could close the door.

"Thank you, sir."

"It's not without complications." The commander motioned to a chair at the conference table. "You will have to put in a few weeks sim training before you're allowed back in flight." As Mercer lowered his bag to the floor and sat, the commander continued. "The paperwork will be a slow process. All of the service branches are reorganizing while the Unified States focuses on rebuilding infrastructure, but we need pilots. You were declared M.I.A. after the incident at McMurdo

Station and now you are being hailed a hero for capturing one of our nation's biggest enemies."

Mercer shook his head. "I didn't exactly capture Volt, sir."

"Well, it was the signal you sent from the icebreaker that led us to him. How you survived on a dinghy for a month while you waited for help is beyond me, and the look of that storm behind you when they pulled you from the water!" The commander shivered. "It's a sight I won't soon forget. But the important thing is, you kept yourself off the boat while Volt and his men died of that awful disease."

While the commander spoke, Mercer thought of his month—not on the dinghy like he had reported, but in the village of Good Springs in the Land. He had spent the past four months on the carrier thinking of little else: the Land's beautiful terrain, the pristine fresh water, and the antiquated lifestyle that made him want to leave. When he reminisced about toying with the affections of the cute virgin, Bethany, he considered his time in the Land better than a month drifting at sea, but when he thought of the backbreaking work on Everett's farm and the cultural restrictions of their society, he recanted his former summation.

"And you never had any symptoms?" the commander asked.

Mercer remembered every moment of his experience with the deadly disease from when the fever gripped him to waking up on the shore of the Land. As he thought of the suffocating burn inside his lungs before he drank Lydia's gray leaf tea, he cleared his throat and looked the commander in the eye. "None, sir."

The commander nodded at him and then sat in the chair at the opposite end of the table. "When the plague hit us, the carrier lost half her crew within a month—three thousand men and women dead. It was the single greatest tragedy I witnessed during the war. But it's behind us now." The commander leaned back in his chair. "Countries can't fight when most of their people are sick or dead. The war is over and the Unified States is rebuilding, albeit with a fraction of her former population. And you will be the guest of honor at the admiral's banquet this Saturday. Your mother is being flown to Norfolk as we speak."

Mercer shook his head, believing the commander was mistaken. "It can't be my mother, sir. None of my family survived the water poisoning."

"Your mother did. She was surprised to learn you had survived the war and the plague—not many did." As Mercer processed the news of his mother's survival, the commander stood and stepped to the door. "We disembark at zero nine hundred."

"Thank you, sir." Mercer lifted his bag to his shoulder as he rose. "I look forward to it."

Thank you for reading my book. I'm so glad you went on this journey with me. More Uncharted stories await you! Are you ready for the adventure?

I know it's important for you to enjoy these wholesome, inspirational stories in your favorite format, so I've made sure all of my books are available in large print.

Below is a quick description of each story so you can determine which books to order next…

**The Uncharted Series**
A hidden land settled by peaceful people ~ The first outsider in 160 years

*The Land Uncharted* (#1)
Lydia's secluded society is at risk when an injured fighter pilot's parachute carries him to her hidden land.

*Uncharted Redemption* (#2)
When vivacious Mandy is forced to depend on strong, silent Levi, she must learn to accept tender love from the one man who truly knows her.

*Uncharted Inheritance* (#3)
Bethany and Everett belong together, but when a mysterious man arrives in the Land, everything changes.

*Christmas with the Colburns* (#4)
When Lydia faces a gloomy holiday in the Colburn house, an unexpected gift brightens her favorite season.

*Uncharted Hope* (#5)
While Sophia and Nicholas wrestle with love and faith, a stunning discovery outside the Land changes everything.

*Uncharted Journey* (#6)
When horse trainer Solo moves to Falls Creek, widow Eva gets a second chance at love. Meanwhile, Bailey's quest to reach the Land costs her everything.

*Uncharted Destiny* (#7)
The Uncharted story continues when Bailey and Revel face an impossible rescue mission in the Land's treacherous mountains.

*Uncharted Promises* (#8)

When Sybil and Isaac get snowed in, it takes more than warm meals and cozy fireplaces to help them find love at the Inn at Falls Creek.

*Uncharted Freedom* (#9)
When Naomi takes the housekeeping job at The Inn at Falls Creek so she can hide from one past, another finds her.

*Uncharted Courage* (#10)
With the survival of the Land at stake and their hearts on the line, Bailey and Revel must find the courage to love.

**The Uncharted Beginnings Series**
Embark on an unforgettable 1860s journey with the Founders as they discover the Land.

*Aboard Providence* (#1)
When Marian and Jonah's ship gets marooned on a mysterious uncharted island, they must build a settlement to survive. Love and adventure await!

*Above Rubies* (#2)
When schoolteacher Olivia needs the settlement elders' approval, she must hide her dyslexia from everyone, even charming carpenter Gabe.

*All Things Beautiful* (#3)
Henry is the last person Hannah wants reading her story… and the first person to awaken her heart.


Find out more on my website keelybrookekeith.com or feel free to email me at keely@keelykeith.com where I answer every message personally.

See you in the Land!
Keely

# About Keely Brooke Keith

Keely Brooke Keith writes inspirational frontier-style fiction with a futuristic twist, including *The Land Uncharted* (Shelf Unbound Notable Romance 2015) and *Aboard Providence* (2017 INSPY Awards Longlist).

Born in St. Joseph, Missouri, Keely was a tree-climbing, baseball-loving 80s kid. She grew up in a family who moved often, which fueled her dreams of faraway lands. When she isn't writing, Keely enjoys teaching home school lessons and playing bass guitar. Keely, her husband, and their daughter live on a hilltop south of Nashville, Tennessee.

# Acknowledgements

My heartfelt gratitude goes to my patient and supportive family, friends, and encouragers. Some of you bolstered me through this entire journey; some of you simply spoke a word of encouragement that spurred me on in a tough moment. There are so many who've encouraged me that I failed to note, and as soon as this goes to press I will probably remember your help and have a big face-palm moment, but here is my best shot…

Thanks Marty Keith, Rachel Keith, Pam Heckman, Rod Heckman, Karen Lawler, Amber Barron, Christina Yother, Annalise Hulsey, Claribel Ortega, Jennifer Cortez, Megan Easley-Walsh, Vickie Pantle, Ana Klundt, Ron Wilcoxson, Tamera Alexander, Robin, Cherine, Theola, Melissa, Chad, Sam, Anita, Tamara, Rae, Jared, Nicole, Blake,

Lynette, Kent, Michelle, Joel, Carolyn, Kelly, Margaret, Angela, Jacob, Brenda, Sharon, Kathryn, Frank, Dena, Najla, Fellowship Bible Church worship team friends, Inside Edits, and the Clean Indie Reads tribe.

Made in the USA
Monee, IL
22 March 2023

30297511R00246